To Roosevelt Library
in honor of
Max Banks.

June 16, 1993

THE MACMILLAN BOOK OF
BASEBALL STORIES

THE MACMILLAN BOOK OF
BASEBALL STORIES

by Terry Egan, Stan Friedmann, and Mike Levine

YPX317749/ 796.357
EGA

MACMILLAN PUBLISHING COMPANY NEW YORK

MAXWELL MACMILLAN CANADA TORONTO

MAXWELL MACMILLAN INTERNATIONAL
NEW YORK OXFORD SINGAPORE SYDNEY

Photo credits: pages 17, 24, 49, 90, 105, 115, 121, 125 courtesy of UPI/Reuters Photo Libraries; pages 28, 30 courtesy of State of New York Executive Chambers; page 36 courtesy of National Baseball Library, Cooperstown, N.Y. (Luis Ramos, photographer); page 43 courtesy of the Oakland Tribune/Matthew J. Lee; pages 52, 57, 68–69, 101, 118 courtesy of National Baseball Library, Cooperstown, N.Y.; page 63 courtesy of the New York Yankees/Andre Adelson; pages 78, 79 courtesy of Brooklyn Public Library, Brooklyn Collection, Brooklyn Eagle Collection; pages 82–83 courtesy of AP/World Wide Photos; page 92 courtesy of Artist's Proof, Washington, D.C.; page 95 courtesy of Phil Kamrass.

The quotation on page 59 is from "Hub Fans Bid Kid Adieu" by John Updike.

Macmillan books are available at special discounts for bulk purchases for sales promotions, premiums, fund-raising, or educational use. For details, contact:

Special Sales Director
Macmillan Publishing Company
866 Third Avenue
New York, NY 10022

Printed in the United States of America

3   5   7   9   10   8   6   4   2

The text of this book is set in 12 pt. Aster.

Library of Congress Cataloging-in-Publication Data

Egan, Terry.
    The Macmillan book of baseball stories / by Terry Egan, Stan Friedmann, and Mike Levine. — 1st ed.
        p.   cm.
    Summary: A collection of true baseball stories featuring players from different eras, teams, and leagues and focusing on human interest and character.
    ISBN 0-02-733280-2
    1. Baseball—United States—Miscellanea—Juvenile literature. [1. Baseball—Miscellanea.] I. Friedmann, Stan. II. Levine, Mike. III. Title.
GV863.A1E38   1992   92-6447

To our children
Terry, Joe, Luke,
Paul, Matthew, Sara,
Ben, Sam,
and to children of all ages

ACKNOWLEDGMENTS

This labor of love was achieved only because the following people pitched in. We gratefully offer our thanks:

To our editor, Harold Underdown, who respects both children and authors.

To our researcher, Mary Flannery Climes, and the helpful folks at the Thrall Library in Middletown, N.Y. We are also indebted to Pat Kelly at the Hall of Fame Library in Cooperstown, to Donna Daley at the Bettman Archives, to Judith Walsh at the Brooklyn Public Library and to Donna Egan, ace transcriber. To Jeff Idelson of the Yankees and to New York Yankee photographer Bob Adamenko who opened many doors for us.

To those who helped these rookie authors find their way in the publishing world—Roger Egan, Tina Carver, Myron Kaplan, Fran Freedman, Charlie McDade.

To our wives—Cathie, Linda, and Lorraine—and to our entire families for their patience and support. The same goes for our friends at *The Times Herald-Record*.

To all the ballplayers who were generous with their stories. To Governor Mario Cuomo and to Bruce Nelson for sharing pages from their childhoods. To the Reverend William Davidson of the Christ Church in Riverdale, N.Y. for his cooperation.

A tip of the cap to our childhood inspirations—Pete Hamill and the late Jimmy Cannon.

A special appreciation to Coach Lou Zaklin. As he has done for generations of children, he helped us find the heart of baseball.

CONTENTS

4 HARD TIMES

5 THE JOY OF THE GAME

INTRODUCTION

There are plenty of baseball books out there, some only for kids, and others just for adults. This book is special—the whole family can enjoy it and learn from it.

As a former big leaguer, I know these stories ring true. I pitched against some of the sluggers you'll read about here—greats like Willie Mays, Ernie Banks, and Mike Schmidt. I've heard stories in the clubhouse about Lou Gehrig and Cool Papa Bell and Ted Williams. It's good to see these stories make baseball history come alive again for children and their parents. And I was surprised to learn new things about these well-known players.

But I treasure this book even more as a parent and as someone who has been involved in Little League baseball. You see, these are more than just great baseball tales. They are stories about people who happen to be baseball players, but who are mainly decent human beings with problems just like anyone else.

These stories are about *real* heroes. Ernie Banks was a great home run hitter, and there's a story in that. But as told here, there's more to the man than baseball. He also overcame the hurdles of poverty to reach the majors and bring joy to the ballpark whenever he played. Ken Griffey, Sr. and Ken Griffey, Jr. playing in the same major league outfield is more than just a baseball novelty. In this telling, it's the happy completion of a game of catch between father and son that began years earlier in their Cincinnati backyard, and a story that also tells of the hard work that made their achievements possible.

As a child, I always enjoyed reading about baseball heroes. I think kids today deserve the same opportunity. It would be a shame if all they heard about were the troublemakers. Here, they can read about the baseball greats who stood tall for their beliefs and their communities, players who made the most of the talents they were born with. They aren't perfect, mind you, just people who tried to do the right thing.

This book is also about fun. I remember playing Little League baseball as a young boy and all the fun and excitement I had during those years. As I look back I cherish the memories of what my dad, Tommy John, Sr., did to make those years so enjoyable. Somehow, we had fun and still learned to play baseball. When I got out of baseball after twenty-six years in the major leagues, I started to coach Little League teams with my wife Sally. I tried to do what my Dad did back in 1953–55: have fun.

And we did something else. Each year after we picked our team we would hold workouts almost every day. I am a firm believer in the work ethic, even at the Little League level. Kids have more fun if they know how to play baseball well. If they know the fundamentals, they stand a better chance to win, and also to feel good about how they played.

I also believe that every game you play should be played with the intent to win. *But* you should know that winning is not all there is and that losing is not the end. Learn from the losses and make your team better by improving what went wrong last time. Win graciously and lose with your head high. You'll see the players in these stories doing just that.

Sally and I got the parents involved. We would tell them what was expected of the kids (to be on time and hustle), and that we wanted to win, but that we wanted to have fun, too. We also asked them to continue with coaching and practice at home. We had as many team parties as we could fit into the schedule. We felt the parties brought the players *and* parents closer together.

Baseball is a fun game. Little League can be fun, too, if the coach includes the parents in the activities of the team. I am a big advocate of Little League baseball—all four of our kids played it, and two million kids worldwide can't be wrong—and I like to see it played in the right spirit. The stories in this book help illustrate what that spirit is. I believe it will be passed on as long as there are good-hearted people playing the game.

Tommy John
(26 years pitching in the majors,
with 288 career wins, 46 career shutouts;
1992 Florida High School Coach of the Year)

1

WE ARE FAMILY

LIKE FATHER, LIKE SON: THE GRIFFEYS

On a chilly April morning in 1976, seven-year-old Ken Griffey, Jr., was playing catch with his dad.

"Hey, Pops, throw me some more grounders," said young Ken.

His dad, All Star outfielder for the world champion Cincinnati Reds, fired a hard bouncer to the boy's left. The boy lunged with his outstretched glove and snared it.

For millions of kids, the first day of a new baseball season is magical. Families everywhere rediscover the simple joy of playing catch, as generations share this springtime celebration on playing fields across America.

"Hey, that's not a bad catch, son," said Ken senior.

The boy couldn't hide his proud smile. "C'mon, Dad, throw me another."

The next grounder hit a pebble and took a bad bounce. Junior bobbled it once, picked it up, and dropped it again. He grabbed it once more but as he was about to throw, the ball slipped out of his hand and rolled down his arm.

"Bet you can't do that again," joked his father.

They both nearly fell down laughing on the new grass. Dad had always told his boy that the best thing about playing baseball was having fun.

After a few more throws, Junior's mom, Birdie, called out into the backyard, "Time for breakfast, fellas." Father and son rushed inside, sweaty and dirty, still laughing about the muffed grounder. Dad and Birdie cooked up some eggs and toast for Junior and his little brother, Craig.

"Dad, can we go to the ballpark with you today?" asked Ken junior.

"If it's okay with Mom," said his father.

Mrs. Griffey smiled and said, "Well, I guess we could find our way out there."

Junior loved going out to Riverfront Stadium, where the Reds played. He'd watch the big crowd file in and listen to the vendors yelling, "Get your scorecard!" and smell the hot dogs sizzling on the grill. He'd pound his glove hoping a foul ball would come his way.

This day, his dad invited him out to the field where the players were warming up. Again father and son played catch. Dad threw some grounders and the boy gobbled up nearly every one. Ken senior introduced his son to some of his Reds teammates—catcher Johnny Bench, first baseman Tony Perez, second baseman Joe Morgan.

"Hey, son," asked Perez, "you wanna be a ballplayer one day like your dad?"

Junior blushed. "Only if that's what he wants," said his father.

Many seasons passed. Father and son kept playing the game they loved. Dad continued to be a major league star. He traveled from town to town far away from home. Ken junior didn't get to play catch with his dad as much as he wanted. He missed him.

The boy rode his dirt bike and went skateboarding. To his mother's horror, he liked collecting worms and leaving them in his pockets. What he loved most, though, was playing baseball. He would throw the ball around with his younger brother, Craig. He played ball with Pete Rose's son, Pete junior, and with Tony Perez's kids, Victor and Eduardo. Ken's mom took him to play in Little League games. He

All those backyard catches pay off. Ken Griffey, Jr.'s amazing catch at Yankee Stadium brings father and son together again.

wished his father could watch him play, especially when he had a great game.

"Dad, guess what?" he shouted to his father over the phone. "I had three hits today."

"That's great, son," said his dad. "You just go out there and enjoy yourself. That's the best part of baseball." Ken Griffey, Sr., missed watching his boy play.

The more baseball Ken junior played, the better he became. His left arm uncorked powerful throws. Soon he was belting baseballs over fences on high school fields. His brother, Craig, and his mom always came to watch him play. One day men with clipboards came to watch young Ken and take notes. They were major league scouts.

At the age of seventeen, Ken Griffey, Jr., signed with the Seattle Mariners. He went to play on the Mariners' Bellingham, Washington, farm team. He was away from home for the first time and he was a little scared. He missed his family. He just wanted to be in the backyard having a catch with his dad.

For the first time in his life, Ken junior stopped having fun playing baseball. He fell into a horrible slump, batting only .230. Everyone was on his case, even his dad. He felt like his father was looking at him as a ball player and not as a son. Finally, his mom came to visit. His dad, playing in Cincinnati, called again. He had thought it over.

"Son, I know what it's like being homesick. I miss you and mom and Craig a lot. We'll all be together soon. Now, don't worry about a thing. Just go out and enjoy yourself."

Ken took his dad's advice. The next day, the boy's season turned around. He began pounding the ball. By the end of the summer, his batting average zoomed one hundred points.

The next year, Ken Griffey, Jr., still only a teenager, made the big league club. He dazzled fans with his speed, his power, and most of all, his love of the game.

In 1990, young Ken got off to a great start, leading the American League in hitting. His dad's Cincinnati Reds were on a roll, too. They talked often on the phone, sharing their good news. More than anything, the son wished his father could watch him play.

On April 26 Ken junior was standing in center field in Yankee Stadium. His Mariners were playing the Bronx Bombers. It was the bottom of the fourth. Yankee Jesse Barfield blasted a fastball into left center field, the deepest part of the stadium. Everyone in the ballpark thought it would be a home run.

Ken wouldn't give up. He raced back, legs churning, his eye on the ball. Back, back, back to the warning track. He dug his right cleat halfway up the eight-foot wall. He leaped. As the ball disappeared into the night, Griffey flung his arm over the center field fence.

When he came back down he held his glove high above his head. The ball was tucked safely in his mitt. Without breaking stride, he headed toward the Mariners' dugout, holding the final out of the inning.

At first the Yankee fans were silent in disbelief. Then they rose to their feet, thundering applause upon the young ballplayer from the opposing team. Ken junior broke into a big smile. He waved his glove at a distant figure in the stands. His father waved back.

The elder Griffey had flown to New York on his day off to see his son play. After the game, a mob of reporters gathered around Junior to ask about his spectacular catch. They were hanging on his every word. Here was a young sensation, hitting close to .400, stealing bases, banging home runs.

"What's your secret?" the writers asked Ken Griffey, Jr.

He shrugged his shoulders and said, "I guess I have fun playing baseball."

His father was standing in the locker room watching him. Junior looked up and saw his dad.

"Hey," Dad told his son, "that wasn't a bad . . ."

Nothing more was said. They stood there for a long moment and smiled at each other. That night they had dinner together. Then Dad had to catch a plane to rejoin the Reds.

"See you soon," said his dad.

Junior continued to star for the Mariners. He talked to his father on the telephone when they could. After one of those conversations, Ken Griffey, Sr., had an idea.

On the last day of August 1990, Ken junior trotted out to center field for the start of a game against the Kansas City Royals. Jogging alongside him was the left fielder. Ken junior felt a tingle of excitement down his back. The new left fielder was none other than his dad.

They were major league teammates. Ken senior had given up his chance to play on a championship team in order to play alongside his son. The crowd at the Seattle Kingdome let out a roar. This was the first time in history that a father and son had played on the same team. The two started warming up, throwing the ball back and forth. It seemed so familiar, yet so new. Ken junior looked up into the stands and saw his mom. The young man was so happy. I feel like crying, the center fielder thought to himself.

In the bottom of the first inning, the Mariners came up to bat. With one out, Ken senior stepped into the batter's box. On deck was Ken junior. A thought crossed his mind: Wouldn't it be great if Dad got on base and I was able to drive him home? He started laughing.

Suddenly Junior piped up, "Come on, Dad!"

Ken senior heard him. He began laughing so hard, he had to step out of the batter's box. He had never heard "Come on, Dad" before in the major leagues. No one had. Even the guys in the dugout were laughing.

Griffey stepped back in to hit, and Kansas City pitcher Storm Davis threw him a fastball. He punched it past the second baseman for a single.

With his dad on first, Ken junior came up to bat. He lined a single to center, sending Dad to second. The bases were full of Griffeys. They both came around to score that inning as the Mariners breezed to a 5–2 victory.

Microphones and cameras surrounded the Griffeys in the clubhouse. And when later that month father and son hit back-to-back homers, they were the talk of America. The Griffeys were invited to appear on TV shows. President George Bush sent them a telegram of congratulations.

They were grateful for the honors they received and knew that in some way their lives had changed forever. They also realized that what was most important to them hadn't changed at all. Once again, father and son were playing catch, as they have throughout the years on fields across America.

POPS' FAMILY: THE 1979 PITTSBURGH PIRATES

Pops saw it.

His team was down. Some players were injured; others squawked about not getting enough playing time. Everyone was blaming someone else for the Pirates' poor start.

It was only May, but if the Pittsburgh Pirates continued like this—twenty-five people going in twenty-five different directions—they'd be out of the pennant race by Memorial Day.

Something had to be done, and there was only one man to do it.

Willie "Pops" Stargell called a team meeting. A Pirate for seventeen years of his major league career, Pops was the team leader. The younger players looked up to him like a father.

It wasn't just because he was the Pirates' greatest home run hitter ever. He knew what being a team member was all about, that it was just like being part of a family. His parents had told him that families who stuck together could overcome all obstacles. They said, the whole world was family.

So was a baseball team, figured Stargell. That's what I have to tell the guys. Now thirty-eight years old and in the twilight of his career, Stargell wanted to pass the message of family on to the younger Bucs.

The players gathered around him.

A team shouldn't be pointing fingers at each other, he said. When times are bad, that's when you really have to pull together. "We're all one family. Come on. Now let's go out and play together and have some fun."

The Pirates listened to Pops. Playing as a real team, they went on a tear against the rest of the National League. Stargell led the way, banging home runs. Teammate Dave Parker was bashing the ball, too.

Newcomers Tim Foli and Bill Madlock became the glue that held the Pirates' infield together.

Mike Easler and Bill Robinson took turns playing left field. Neither one of them had ever had a great year by themselves, but together, they gave the Pirates the most potent left field in baseball.

Every player on the team accepted his role as a "family" member. Rennie Stennett had once been an All Star second baseman. Manager Chuck Tanner now started Phil Garner ahead of Stennett, who was slowed by injuries. Stennett didn't sulk; he cheered Garner on. When called up to pinch-hit, Stennett always seemed to keep a rally going.

They all began to see themselves as a family.

Soon these Pirates were adopted by the whole city. Fans flocked to see their family play. Stargell helped keep the spirit going by having a popular song of the day blared over the public address system. During the games the whole ballpark sang "We Are Family."

The song spilled over into the streets and gave the city a lift.

When the Pirates needed an extra spark, the fans would start singing, "We are family. Come on, everybody, and dance."

Soon it became the theme song for the entire city of Pittsburgh, a city Stargell loved.

The Pirates battled the Montreal Expos in a thrilling division race. During the final three weeks of the season, the lead changed hands nine times.

The Family embraces Pops Stargell as he arrives safe at home.

When it was all over, the Pirates were standing on top. In the league championship series they rolled over the Cincinnati Reds.

What was once just a collection of twenty-five unhappy ballplayers was now a close-knit family. Pops and the Pirates were going to play the Baltimore Orioles in the World Series.

The Series started, and the Pirates fell on their faces. Over the first three games, they lost twice, making errors and base-running mistakes. In the fourth game, with a chance to tie the Series at home, they wasted a Willie Stargell homer and blew a three-run lead.

They were down three games to one. You could hear a pin drop in Pittsburgh.

Heads down, the Pirates filed into the clubhouse. Reporters pounced on them. "Have you given up?" they asked. "Is the Pirate 'family' falling apart? Do you realize only three teams in Series history have ever come back after being down three games to one?"

Downcast, the Pirates searched for answers. They looked to Pops. The slugging first baseman sat in front of his locker, calmly eating a customary postgame snack.

"Things look bad," a reporter said to Stargell. "You must be real down."

"Me?" Stargell responded in a voice loud enough for the whole team to hear. "I'm playing in the World Series and I'm having fun. Losing a ball game doesn't change that. All we need are three one-game winning streaks. Tomorrow we're going to go out and have a good time playing baseball."

As Stargell's words filled the room, the cloud of doom lifted. "Yeah, that's right," his teammates repeated. "All we need are three one-game winning streaks." Music blared, laughter echoed. The clubhouse became a fun house again.

The Pirates won the next two games to tie the series at three games. It was down to one final game.

The Orioles took a 1–0 lead. Pittsburgh couldn't get anything going against starter Scott McGregor.

The game crept into the sixth inning, the Pirates still down 1–0. With two out and a man on first, Stargell was due up. McGregor had fooled him badly his first two times at bat. Pops listened as batting coach Bob Skinner reminded him to be patient. His teammate Manny Sanguillen lent him his special bat.

McGregor threw Stargell a fastball high and tight. Ball one. In came another heater, up and in. Ball two.

Stargell figured McGregor was setting him up for a breaking ball. He remembered what he had told his "family" all year: Be patient. Don't get tense and overanxious. Relax.

McGregor threw the next pitch. It was that curveball, all right. Stargell waited on it perfectly. He connected. The ball sailed high and deep. Right fielder Ken Singleton ran back to the fence. Stargell watched him leap, his body draping over the fence, glove outstretched. The ball landed just beyond Singleton's glove in the Pirate bull pen.

Home run!

The Bucs were ahead, 2–1. In the dugout, the "family" pounded Pops with joy.

The Pirates held that lead for dear life. Finally, in the ninth, Kent Tekulve shut the Orioles down for good.

The Pirates were world champs.

The family embraced, jumping up and down. They had done the near impossible. In the clubhouse, the beat thumped louder than ever. "We are family. Come on, everybody, and dance."

Pops savored every minute of it. In the Series he had batted .400. His three home runs and four doubles set a World Series record for extra base hits.

As reporters gathered around, a happy Stargell had one more score to settle. The Bucs had taken plenty of ribbing for calling themselves a family. One Baltimore columnist made fun of them, noting that none of the Pirates were actually related to each other. They came from different countries, had different skin colors, different mothers and fathers.

"Yes, we are family," said Pops. "We depend on each other. We lean on each other in hard times. We work hard. We have fun together. If that's not real family, what is?"

MARIO AND HIS FIELDS OF DREAMS

Mario's parents sailed from Salerno, Italy, in search of the great America. They found it in 1925. As their boat passed the Statue of Liberty, they saw in the distance the busy avenues of New York City.

Maybe the streets weren't paved with gold, but the parents believed this was the land of opportunity. Through study and hard work, a poor man's child could become a doctor, a judge, even a governor.

Mario's father dug ditches. He sold fruit from a pushcart. He saved pennies and opened a small grocery store in the south Jamaica neighborhood of Queens.

Mario was the second of three children. He saw how hard his parents worked, sunup to sundown. Every day they told him, "Study. Study hard. You can be somebody. There is a place for you in the great American dream."

Mario was a good student. He enjoyed learning. What he really loved, though, was the great American game: baseball. It was all around him, in the streets of New York, in the crackling sounds of Dodger broadcasts on the family radio, in the Polo Grounds, at Ebbetts Field, and Yankee Stadium, the homes of New York's teams.

After school he'd roam the playgrounds of Queens, playing center field. Whether he was sliding into second base to break up a double

Little Mario and his proud immigrant family stand outside their grocery store.

play or sprinting back for fly balls, Mario played hard, real hard.

He was a teenager when he played for a traveling team from his neighborhood. They went to Fort Monmouth, New Jersey, to play a game against a special services team of army ballplayers. The pitcher was Whitey Ford, the rookie sensation from the New York Yankees.

Watching on the sidelines was Pittsburgh Pirates scout Ed McCarric. He couldn't take his eyes off the young center fielder. The kid could hit and throw and run. After the game McCarric told Mario he wanted to sign him up.

McCarric said he'd give Mario a $2,000 signing bonus. Mario couldn't believe it. That was a ton of money. Mickey Mantle only got $1,100 to sign with the Yankees a few years before.

He couldn't wait to get home to tell his father. Because he was underage—still in high school—he needed his father to sign the contract. He was certain his dad would.

His folks worked hard. They could use the money. And Mario would get to play baseball. He saw this as a road to his great American dream.

His father shook his head. "Don't they play baseball in the summer, before school ends?" he asked.

"Well, yeah, Pops, but—"

"No," said his father. "Absolutely not."

Mario couldn't believe it. McCarric couldn't believe it. He begged Branch Rickey, the Pirates president, not to let this kid get away. He could be the best prospect in the whole organization.

If there was one thing Branch Rickey valued in this world, it was baseball talent. Just five years earlier he had signed up Jackie Robinson, who became the major leagues' first African-American ball player.

All Rickey cared about was whether a kid could play ball. Mario could, and Rickey wanted him. He wrote a personal letter to Mario's father: "I admire you for wanting your child to get an education. And as head of this outfit, I can promise you that your son will not have to play ball for us until after his classes end."

His father still wasn't convinced. He was worried his son would forget about college and only care about baseball.

Mario was desperate. He wanted to play ball so badly, but he knew he had to listen to his father.

McCarric paid a personal visit to the family grocery store. Under

Mario pursues his American dream.

the hanging sticks of provolone and salami, McCarric pleaded with Mario's father: "Don't worry, we'll make sure he doesn't touch a baseball until his classes are over."

The father looked at Mario. "Do you promise you'll stay with your education and that you'll go to college?"

"Yes, Pops. I give you my word."

His father signed the contract.

In 1952, after graduating from high school, Mario reported to the minor league Brunswick Pirates in Georgia. He played center field. He hit okay: .252. He showed a lot of power. He played hard. He noticed how good the rest of the players were and how hard he would have to work to make it to the major leagues. But he loved it.

Then, during a game late in the season, Mario ran into trouble. He had gotten two hits off a pitcher named Ed Barbier. The next time up, Barbier meant to brush Mario back from the plate. But the pitch was too far inside. The ball hit Mario in the head.

In the hospital for a month, he had plenty of time to think. He remembered going to Yankee Stadium a few years back to see Joe DiMaggio play. Now, that was a ball player. That was greatness. Sure, Mario loved baseball. But he figured he was never going to be Joe DiMaggio.

Because Mario had studied hard in school, St. John's University in Queens was offering him an academic scholarship. He was all alone with a big decision to make. He thought of baseball and he thought of the promise he had made to his father. Mario decided to drop baseball and his dream of a major league career so that he could go to college.

Mario continued to love the game but he never did go on to play center field for the Pittsburgh Pirates. He probably would have been too busy anyway. On November 5, 1982, Mario M. Cuomo was elected the fifty-second governor of the state of New York.

His father was right about this great country. There is more than one avenue to the American dream.

PAPI AND ROBERTITO: A SON REMEMBERS ROBERTO CLEMENTE

Robertito was so excited, he wore his Little League uniform to bed. Highlights from tomorrow's game danced in his head. He just knew he'd make a sliding catch or hit the game-winning homer. He pictured himself running around the bases with the big number twenty-one on his back, the number worn by his dad, Roberto Clemente. The boy began to think about his father. His dad had told him that, as a kid, he, too, used to think about baseball before he fell asleep. He'd lie in bed bouncing a ball off the wall, listening to it thunk in the darkness.

Robertito's dad loved baseball. His dad told him that as a boy in Puerto Rico, he didn't have a uniform. His dad said he would play on fields thick with mud and spotted with trees. His first bat was made out of a guava-tree branch. His first glove was cut from a coffee-bean sack. His first ball was a knot of rags.

One day, his dad said, he had played in a game that started in the morning and ended at dinnertime. He had hit ten homers.

Wow, thought Robertito, turning in his bed, that must have been incredible. Robertito knew his dad had played so well that there were stories the whole world had heard. Stories that began before the boy was even born. Like when his dad was nineteen and Branch Rickey came to Puerto Rico to watch him play. Rickey, considered baseball's greatest talent scout, had heard Roberto Clemente could do it all. He could run. He could hit. And could he ever throw.

During the practice before the game, Rickey saw young Clemente make an awesome running catch in right field, then turn and fire a strike to home plate. Rickey asked to talk to the young player.

"Like baseball, son?" Rickey asked.

"More than eating, sir," Roberto Clemente said.

"Young man," Rickey declared, "you're going to be a superstar."

Two years later Clemente was playing right field for the Pittsburgh Pirates. With Clemente in right, the Pirates boasted the strongest arm in the game. Runners wouldn't dare go from first to third on a single. At bat, Clemente would smash line drives all over the ballpark.

The Pirates were a terrible team when Clemente arrived. Five years later, in 1960, they were world champions.

The 1960s was Clemente's decade. He won four batting titles, he made the All Star team nearly every year, and in 1966 he was voted the league's Most Valuable Player.

That wasn't even the highlight of his year. On August 17, 1966, his first son was born. He and his wife named him Roberto Clemente, Jr.

"Robertito," his dad would call him, bouncing the baby on his knee.

Robertito was his daddy's pride and joy. The boy was crazy about his father, too. Robertito would crawl from room to room following his dad. And when Roberto Clemente went away to play baseball, his son couldn't wait for him to come home to Puerto Rico.

When he did, he would tuck Robertito into bed and tell him baseball stories. The father thought about the time his son would be old enough to have a catch with him. He knew Robertito would have all the things he never had as a kid—a real glove, new bats, a nice field, and a uniform.

Roberto wished he could do the same for every kid in Puerto Rico. He made up his mind that he would try. Roberto Clemente pictured a place with baseball fields and playgrounds and lakes nearby where fathers and sons could spend time together fishing. It would be called Sports City and it would be Roberto Clemente's gift to the children of Puerto Rico and the world.

Each spring Clemente would return to Pittsburgh to play right field for the Pirates. Many times, he brought Robertito along. Before the games, when the father would trot out to right field in an empty ballpark, Robertito would follow in his footsteps. He'd watch as his dad got ready to play by bouncing a ball off the outfield wall.

"Papi, what are you doing that for?" Robertito asked.

"Being good takes hard work and desire," said the father.

All that hard work and desire paid off in 1971 when Roberto Clemente led his Pirates to the World Championship. People still say no one ever played a better Series than Clemente. He hit, he threw, he ran with perfection. The Puerto Rican kid who learned to hit a baseball with a guava-tree branch had become America's biggest baseball hero.

There was no bigger welcome for Clemente than in Puerto Rico. He was mobbed by thousands of young fans who showed up to greet his plane.

He was happy to be home so that he could spend time with his children. That was great news for Robertito and his two little brothers. When he heard his dad had to go out of town, the boy would hide his father's airplane tickets.

Come spring, Clemente went to play for the Pirates again. He sent for his wife and children to come visit him. On the last day of the 1972 season, Robertito watched his dad bounce a double off the wall in left center field. It was his three thousandth hit; only Hall of Famers ever hit that many.

The crowd stood up and cheered for Roberto Clemente. Willie

Mays trotted over from the Mets dugout and shook his hand. Nobody was prouder than Robertito. After the game the Clementes went back to Puerto Rico. Roberto planned on opening a free medical clinic, and he began looking for sites for Sports City, his gift to children. Robertito was proud of that, too, and he was glad to have his father home for the winter.

That fall Roberto managed a Puerto Rican team in a November tournament in Nicaragua. Roberto met many friends there, including a poor boy who was missing a leg. Roberto Clemente arranged to get him an artificial leg.

Nicaragua was still fresh in Clemente's mind when it was leveled by an earthquake a month later. He cried when he heard more than six thousand people had been killed, many of them children. Thousands more were injured and homeless. From Puerto Rico, Clemente led relief efforts sending food to Nicaragua. On Christmas morning Clemente's own gifts remained unopened as he worked tirelessly at a San Juan baseball stadium collecting food and loading trucks. Clemente feared for the safety of his friends in Nicaragua. He wondered if the hospital still stood. Was his young friend with the artificial leg still alive?

Two days before the New Year, Roberto sat in the family dining room explaining to his wife why he had to go to Nicaragua. "I have to make sure the supplies are getting to the people," he said.

Six-year-old Robertito remembers walking into the dining room. "Mommy," he said, "tell Papi not to go. The plane is going to crash."

The next day, on New Year's Eve, Roberto Clemente left on his mission of mercy. He never made it. Shortly after the plane took off, it crashed into the ocean. America had lost one of its greatest baseball players. Puerto Rico had lost a friend and hero. The world had lost a good man.

But Robertito had lost his father. The boy lay in a bed in his Little League uniform, his father's number twenty-one across his back.

Roberto Clemente's Memorial . . . his son says good-bye.

Tomorrow's game would soon begin. He fell asleep at last, dreaming of a baseball streaking across the Puerto Rican sky.

Almost twenty years later, Roberto Clemente, Jr., would stand in a major league uniform, bat in hand, talking about his dad. He'd say how much his father had given him in such a short time, how his father's courage had inspired him, not to play baseball, but to make the most of life. By then, Roberto Clemente, Jr., was wearing a different uniform number. He understood he was his own man.

2

DOING THE RIGHT THING

HOMETOWN HERO: DAVE STEWART AND THE EARTHQUAKE OF '89

People are always popping off about ball players today. They're selfish and only care about money. They don't give a hoot about anyone else.

These people must not know about Dave Stewart.

Sure they know him as a great pitcher for the Oakland Athletics, a hometown kid who made good. They know he won more than twenty games four years in a row and threw a no-hitter in 1990. They know year after year he was overlooked for the Cy Young Award. A lot of people even remember that gem of a shutout he threw in the first game of the 1989 World Series against the San Francisco Giants.

But not many know what Dave Stewart did a few nights later. Game three of the Series was about to start in San Francisco. The A's had won the first two games of the Series against their rivals across the bay. Everyone was talking baseball.

Minutes before the teams were to be introduced to a packed Candlestick Park, a low rumble was heard. The walls of the stadium shook. The seats in the upper deck began to sway. People felt dizzy as the concrete beneath their feet moved. Suddenly, everyone knew.

They were being rocked by an earthquake.

The tremors lasted several frightening moments. Afterward, everything seemed so strange. Police cars circled the field, their red lights flashing. Ball players in search of loved ones wandered around the stadium in their uniforms.

A voice over the loudspeaker told the people not to panic but to leave the stadium and go home. People wondered if they had homes. In San Francisco and across the bay in Oakland, bridges crumbled, houses toppled, and buildings burned.

Dave Stewart left the ballpark in his uniform and went home. He tried to get some sleep, but it was no use. He knew his hometown was burning.

He went out and wandered the city, walking the streets where he grew up. His neighborhood was a hardworking area of crowded row houses called West Oakland. Folks were out on the street, scared of what happened and what might come.

The superstar, who just a few days ago had won game one of the World Series, went house to house to see if people were okay. Did they need anything? Stewart asked. Get in touch with a relative? Check on a loved one? He'd do anything to help.

Stewart walked in a daze. He saw fire trucks streaking by, shrieking in alarm. Something inside tugged at him and he followed the red lights to the Oakland waterfront.

He was stunned. A section of highway had collapsed. People were trapped inside their cars. Rescue workers tried desperately to free them. Heavy sections of concrete had to be lifted by giant cranes. The progress was so slow, inch by inch, and the air was full of sweat and frustration.

Stewart watched the fire fighters and police officers and ambulance workers and construction crews and he knew he could not do what they were doing. But it was his neighborhood, these were his friends, and he had to do something.

Without thinking, Stewart became part of the rescue team. The million-dollar pitcher ran errands, got coffee. He talked to rescue

Dave Stewart — as kind off the mound as he is competitive on it.

workers, encouraging them to push on, reminding them how much their town needed them.

It was a horrible, endless night but the rescue workers saved many lives. They later said Stewart's encouragement inspired them. Here was a big star who cared so much about his hometown, he couldn't sleep in its moment of need.

He was hailed as one of the shining lights of that dark night.

"I still don't feel like a hero," Stewart said later. "If that's the case, there are a lot of other people who are bigger heroes than me. Everybody just came together."

For the next several nights, rescuers picked through the rubble of toppled buildings and collapsed bridges. Stewart was there to lend a hand.

And when the Series resumed ten days later, Stewart was still working for his hometown of Oakland. He was the starting pitcher in game three and he shut down the Giants again. He was the Series Most Valuable Player (MVP) and he finally won the Cy Young Award as his league's best pitcher.

America started to look at Stewart as more than just a great athlete. It discovered that for years he had quietly given himself to his community, working for charities such as the Boys Club, the United Way, and the Cystic Fibrosis Foundation. He had sponsored activities for kids, dance troupes, and a girls' track team.

To Stewart, it was just a matter of giving back to his hometown.

The community appreciated it. After the earthquake, a jeweler who had never met Stewart sat down and made a necklace for the pitcher. When it was delivered to Stewart by a sports reporter, Stewart cried. After the World Series he found the jeweler and thanked him.

For all Dave Stewart had done for others, he was given the Roberto Clemente Award. Like the late Clemente, who had given back to his community and who had died trying to help victims of an earthquake, Stewart had never forgotten his roots. He had long admired Clemente. Stewart said the award meant more to him than winning the Cy Young Award or the World Series MVP.

"Clemente was a great, great man," said Stewart.

A couple of years later Stewart was sitting at his locker thinking back on the earthquake. Someone asked him why a rich baseball superstar would toil long nights fetching coffee for rescue workers.

Dave Stewart shrugged and said, "It was the human thing to do."

KOUFAX AND THE KID

Bruce Nelson didn't even want to get on the school bus that morning. Head down, he climbed the steps and looked for an empty seat.

"Hey, Bruce," a friend called from the back, "did you see Kaline's homer last night? The Tigers creamed the Sox."

"Yeah," Bruce said halfheartedly.

Bruce Nelson sat alone. He stared out a window as the bus rolled by Kewpee's burger joint, Muir's soda fountain, the synagogue, all the places that made East Lansing, Michigan, his hometown. And over there on the corner was the little shop where Bob the barber always talked baseball with him.

Suddenly it dawned on Bruce that he wouldn't even get to go to Briggs Stadium anymore, that neat old ballpark in nearby Detroit where his Tigers played. No more would he see his favorite players— Al Kaline, Norm Cash, Mickey Lolich.

Just the night before, Bruce Nelson's father had come home with the news about his new job. "I've got an offer in California," his father said. "I've got to take it. We're moving to Los Angeles."

Bruce wanted to cry and his father saw it. "Hey, Son, they have Disneyland and Hollywood out there and it's summer all the time."

"Yeah," Bruce said, "but they don't have the Tigers."

"That's true," his father said, "but they have the Dodgers. And a pitcher by the name of Sandy Koufax. Wait till you see how fast he throws."

"Koufax," Bruce Nelson thought, looking out the school bus window. "How am I supposed to root for a guy I don't even know?"

Bruce Nelson didn't know it, but just a few years before, Sandy Koufax himself had to make a move to Los Angeles. Koufax had grown up in Brooklyn and his team was the Brooklyn Dodgers. When a Dodgers scout had seen Sandy's blazing fastball, the team signed him. He'd made the team in 1955, at the age of nineteen. He was playing for his hometown and he was happy.

But two years later, the headlines in the New York papers screamed that the Dodgers were leaving for Los Angeles. Koufax would no longer play in his hometown.

The young pitcher hadn't known what to think. His whole life had been in Brooklyn—his family, his pals. But he had no choice. He had to move to Los Angeles.

Bruce Nelson had no choice either. He moved to California with his family. He tried and tried to blend into his new neighborhood but it was tough. He still felt like a stranger. Then one day a kid from the neighborhood asked Bruce if he wanted to go to a Dodgers game.

"It's not Kaline," Bruce thought to himself. "But it would be fun to see a ball game."

He couldn't believe his eyes. The stadium was brand-new and beautiful. The parking lot looked as big as the Grand Canyon. He and his friend found their way to a set of box seats, right behind the Dodgers' dugout.

"Who's pitching today?" Bruce asked his friend.

"Number thirty-two, Sandy Koufax," his friend said. "Houston might as well go home now."

Koufax was tall and graceful but that's not what grabbed Bruce's eye. It was the fastball that seemed to get faster as it approached the plate. The popping sound it made when it smacked into the catcher's glove. It was the curveball that came in so quick and, at the last second, broke over the plate like magic.

"Wow," Bruce said, watching the batters walk helplessly back to the dugout. "What a pitcher. Is he always this good?"

"He's the best," his friend said.

Koufax pitched his team to victory that day, and the Dodgers were one step closer to the National League pennant. Early the next month, Bruce listened on the radio as Koufax threw a perfect game against the Cubs in Chicago. It was the twenty-second win of the season for Koufax. His twenty-sixth would clinch the pennant for the Dodgers.

The Dodgers got ready to play the Minnesota Twins in the World Series. Naturally, Koufax was the Dodgers' choice to start the opening game. But there was a problem. The game was scheduled for Wednesday, October 6. That was the date of the holiest of Jewish holidays, Yom Kippur. It's a day when Jews pray for forgiveness and vow to be better people. So solemn is this day that many Jews do not work or eat or play.

Koufax was Jewish. He had to decide. Should he honor his faith and miss the game? Suppose they lost without him on the mound? What would his teammates think of him? Maybe it would just be better if he blended in and forgot about his faith for one day.

He couldn't. Koufax decided he had to be true to himself and to his beliefs. He told his manager that he couldn't pitch in the opening game of the Series.

Once again Bruce Nelson knew what Koufax was going through. He was going through the same thing himself. He, too, was Jewish. He didn't know whether to go to school on Wednesday like the rest of his classmates. What would he tell them? He was the only one who would be missing. He really wanted to be one of the guys. He wanted to be accepted.

All's well that ends well: Koufax is mobbed by his teammates after he wins the final game of the 1965 World Series.

He could lie. He could tell them he was sick. But then he found out what Koufax was doing. Like Koufax, he observed the holiday on Wednesday. And on Thursday, when his friends asked him where he had been the day before, Bruce Nelson said, "Yesterday was Yom Kippur. It was a Jewish holiday. Koufax didn't pitch and I didn't come to school."

Bruce's classmates, like Koufax's teammates, understood.

Everything worked out okay after all. Koufax, pitching in the seventh and deciding game threw a three-hit shutout. Along with every-one else in Los Angeles, Bruce Nelson celebrated.

His favorite team had won the World Series.

THE COOLEST PAPA EVER

Superman may have been faster than a speeding bullet, but James "Cool Papa" Bell would have beaten him to first base.

How speedy was he? Imagine this:

- He could turn off the light and be in bed before the room got dark.
- Rounding second base one time, he got hit in the leg—with his own line drive.
- He scored all the way from first base on a teammate's sacrifice bunt.
- Leading off first one day, Cool Papa decided to steal a base. By the time the catcher's throw reached second, Cool Papa was sliding into third.
- Another time, Cool Papa caught his own throw from center field and tagged a runner out at third.

Some of these stories are legend but everyone agrees James Bell was one of the greatest players ever. Amazingly, you couldn't find him playing in the major leagues. It didn't matter that he could knock the cover off a ball or that he played the game with smarts and spirit. It didn't even matter that he could run faster than the

Papa's got a brand new bag: Bell flies into third base during a Negro League game.

wind, that he had been timed going around the bases in just twelve seconds.

All that mattered to the people who ran major league baseball was that his skin was black. They wouldn't let him play.

Before 1947 no Americans of African descent were allowed to play major league baseball. Cool Papa Bell had to play in something called the Negro Leagues. It was for blacks only. Bell was one of the league's stars for twenty-four years, hitting over .400 his first year and his last year. He hit over .300 every season.

But here is the most incredible story about Cool Papa Bell. And this time, every word is true.

It happened in 1946, his last year in the Negro Leagues. Cool Papa was forty-three years old and hobbled with arthritis. He was batting an awesome .402 and on the last day of the season he needed just a couple of more at bats to qualify to win the batting title. Not only would it have been the crowning achievement of his career, Bell also stood to earn a bonus for leading the league in hitting. Negro League salaries were pitiful. He could have used the money.

James Bell had one last task to accomplish, which he thought was more important. He knew major league baseball was about to open its doors to black players. Bell knew he was too old to think of a big league career for himself. However, the guy battling Bell for the batting title—a young kid named Monte Irvin—was being considered for the major leagues. If the scouts saw that Irvin won a batting title, they'd be impressed. So Cool Papa Bell sat out that last game and let Irvin win the title. Later, someone asked Bell why he did it.

He answered, "When one of us makes it to the major leagues, we all do." Because Bell opened the door, Monte Irvin was one of the first African Americans allowed to play in the major leagues.

This is the story to remember about James "Cool Papa" Bell.

GOING TO BAT FOR AMERICA: A TIP OF THE CAP TO TED WILLIAMS

They say the only thing Ted Williams cared about in life was hitting a baseball. He'd talk about it, dream about it, show off about it. Even when he came up to his first Boston Red Sox spring training in 1938 at the tender age of nineteen, the sportswriters remarked how cocky Williams was.

The older Red Sox players made fun of him, calling him The Kid. They said he was selfish. The Red Sox outfielders said Williams didn't give a hoot about learning to play the outfield properly. Williams thumbed his nose at them even as he was being sent down to the minors at the end of spring training. He said he'd be back. He swore he'd become a bigger star than all of them put together.

The Kid was right.

Williams came up to the Red Sox for good in 1939. He had the greatest year a rookie ever had, smashing the ball all over Fenway Park and sending his teammates across home plate 145 times.

Unbelievably, he got better. He became Boston's hero. The sportswriters flocked around him, wanting to know all about baseball's hottest hitter. But Williams wouldn't tell them. He didn't want his private life written about. He was distant and rude. He said all he owed Boston fans was his best on the ball field.

The fans cheered him when he did well, but when he didn't hit, they booed him without mercy. Williams sulked. So, when he homered, he refused to tip his cap to the fans, as was the custom of the day.

There goes selfish Ted Williams again, people said. They didn't know that he was really a quiet, private man with a burning desire to succeed. His boasting often covered up his fear of failure. In his own way, he was shy. He would rather have a conversation with a cabdriver than be in the public spotlight. That's the main reason he never told anyone about the charity work he did around Boston or his visits to hospitals to cheer up sick kids.

In 1941 Williams had one of the best years a ball player ever had. On the last day of the season he was hitting .400, an incredible feat achieved by just a few ball players in history. The manager asked Williams if he wanted to sit out the last day so he wouldn't be in danger of falling below .400.

Williams didn't want to be crowned with greatness while he was sitting on the bench. He played every inning of the doubleheader, banging out six hits and finishing the season with a .406 batting average. He is the last player to hit over .400.

After his incredible season, sportswriters didn't even vote him the league's MVP Award. Being the best hitter in baseball simply wasn't enough. Sportswriters and fans continued to find fault with Williams.

In 1942, with World War II raging, hundreds of players went into the armed services. Because Williams was his mother's only son and because he supported her, he didn't have to go.

Typical Ted Williams, the sportswriters wrote, a selfish ball player who puts hitting a baseball above his country.

Williams had another terrific season, winning the Triple Crown by leading the league in home runs, batting average, and runs batted in. Sportswriters again refused to give him the MVP Award.

Williams could have gone on playing baseball, but after the 1942 season he volunteered to fight for his country in the war. Many ball players were fulfilling their wartime duty on service baseball teams, playing exhibition games for the troops.

Ted Williams would have none of that. He used his eagle eyes to become a sharpshooter and an airplane pilot. He sacrificed three of his prime baseball years serving his country.

In 1946 he was back hitting baseballs for the Red Sox. He led his team to another pennant and finally won the MVP Award. He took no bows for his war record. He remained cranky with sportswriters and fans. They were rude to Williams and Williams was rude right back. Once, while rounding the bases after a home run, Williams spit at the press box.

The next year, when Williams won the Triple Crown again, the writers still wouldn't give him the MVP Award.

History always seemed to repeat itself for Ted Williams. In 1952, America was at war again, this time in Korea. Six games into the season, Williams was called up to service. Once again Williams wouldn't take the easy way out. He flew many combat missions over Korea. One day he was fired on by the enemy, 126 bullets piercing his plane and setting it on fire. Williams couldn't eject himself from the plane because his escape system had burned out. The plane's wheels and flaps weren't working either. He had to make a crash landing.

Williams brought the plane in on its belly, hitting the ground at two hundred miles per hour. As soon as he jumped out of the cockpit, the plane burst into flames. He was told to take some time off. But again no one could keep Ted Williams out of the lineup. The next day he was up and flying.

After missing most of the 1952 and 1953 seasons, Williams rejoined the Red Sox. He had lost another huge chunk of his career by serving his country. And now, at thirty-five, he was considered an old baseball player.

War hero Williams gives a thumbs-up to America.

Still, he continued to hit a baseball as well as anyone ever did. He kept his running argument with the press and the fans, who wanted their hero humble and charming. Williams refused to bend, never tipping his cap after a homer. When fans heckled him, he cursed back.

But when no one was looking he could be generous and warm. One day in spring training he heard that a fellow marine wanted to meet him. Williams said sure. He and Ed Bambera, limping and walking with a cane, shook hands. Williams spent lots of time talking with Bambera and, when he found out that Bambera had a serious disease called multiple sclerosis, Williams helped him get proper medical treatment. Williams had Bambera visit him during every spring training after that.

"He's always asking me about my health," Bambera told sportswriters. "Always asking if there isn't something else he can do for me."

By 1959, at the age of forty-one, Williams finally showed his age. He was slowed by injuries and he had the worst season of his career. Everyone figured he'd just quit.

Ted Williams had too much pride to go out with a whimper. He played the 1960 season on pure guts and determination. He had a fine year, too, batting over .300.

On September 28, only 10,453 fans filed into Fenway Park for Ted Williams's last game there. It was a solemn New England afternoon, raw and gray.

His first three times up, the fans cheered and hollered for Williams. But in the eighth inning, when Williams came up for his last at bat, there was only the pure clapping of hands. No hoots or hollers, just waves of applause.

It was a show of respect, the fans' way of saying good-bye to a greatness they did not fully understand. They had realized that perhaps Williams wasn't the selfish man many had suspected. Sure, he could be self-centered and surly, but he had given of himself to his country. He had given of himself to his community. He had given of himself to those in need.

In that last at bat the first pitch to Williams was a low fastball. Williams swung and missed at the second offering. The next pitch came in. Williams connected. He sent the ball rocketing on a high arc toward right center, the deepest part of Fenway. The ball disappeared over the wall—a home run. Writer John Updike was at the game that day. This is how he saw it:

> He ran as he always ran out home runs—hurriedly, unsmiling head down, as if our praises were a storm of rain to get out of. He didn't tip his cap. Though we thumped, wept, chanted "We want Ted" for minutes after he hid in the dugout, he did not come back. . . . The papers said that the other players, and even the umpires on the field, begged him to come out and acknowledge us in some way, but he refused. Gods do not answer letters.

Of course, Ted Williams was not really a god. It turned out he was human like all of us, parts good and bad, easily bruised, full of pride, and hard to understand. And given the chance, inclined to do the right thing.

Long after his playing career was over, Williams was given a special salute at Fenway Park. A whole new generation of fans roared their approval.

Ted Williams, with a shy smile, tipped his cap and waved it to the crowd.

STANDING UP TO THE MONSTER

Sometimes the paths of good people cross.

A five-year-old girl is sitting with her grandfather in Boston's Fenway Park. In the middle of this big city is a pasture of grass and dirt cut in the shape of a diamond. She looks to left field and sees a huge green wall. Her grandfather says, "They call it the Monster."

But not even the Monster seems as awesome as the ball players on the field in front of her. Her seat is so close she can almost touch them. Her eyes settle on one ball player, a tall and angular man with the eyes of an eagle. He picks up a bat and cuts the air with it.

"Who is that?" she asks her grandfather.

"Ted Williams," he says. "Why?"

"Because if God is a person," she says, "that's what he looks like."

That's the day Suzyn Waldman fell in love with baseball.

In Joliet, Illinois, Jesse Barfield is a twelve-year-old kid who loves basketball. His aunt tells him about the game of baseball and a player by the name of Ernie Banks. He's the power-hitting shortstop of the Chicago Cubs, who has a mighty swing and a soft smile. "Ernie loves the game and he loves people," Jesse's aunt tells him.

One day, Jesse's buddy Rich says, "They're having Little League tryouts today. Let's go." Jesse doesn't want to go. His game is hoops, but as a favor to Rich, he goes along.

At the ball field, Jesse discovers he's pretty good at baseball. He has a rifle arm, a powerful swing, and a happy-go-lucky style of play.

Jesse makes the team. His friend doesn't.

Jesse feels terrible. And when some of his teammates fail to show up for practice, Jesse goes to his coach. "It's not fair," he tells his coach. "Rich really wants to play. Can't you let him play?"

The coach agrees. Rich becomes a part of the team.

It wasn't the last time Jesse Barfield would do the right thing in a baseball uniform.

Back in Boston, Suzyn Waldman can't even think of playing Little League baseball. It's the early 1950s and girls aren't allowed.

She's crushed. Her mother tells her to keep on doing her best. Her grandfather knows how much Suzyn loves baseball. He tells her if she keeps on trying, she can do whatever she wants.

She has another love—singing. When she grows up she performs in Broadway shows and in theaters all over the country. And whenever she goes to a different major league city, she goes to the ball park and enjoys her first love—baseball. She even asks to sing "The Star Spangled Banner."

She gets on the field and talks to ball players. One of the broadcasters notices how easily she talks baseball. "You'd make a great broadcaster," he says. That was the first time anyone suggested to Suzyn Waldman that she could do something a woman was never allowed to do.

Over in Joliet, Jesse Barfield is a Little League star. He tears up the Pony League and the Colt League and stars on his high school team. Out of high school he is signed to a contract with the Toronto Blue Jays. Soon he's belting baseballs all over major league parks.

They say he has one of the best arms in the game. He quickly gains a reputation as a hardworking player on the field. Jesse also plays with a lot of joy. He remembers the stories his aunt told him about Ernie Banks. He also remembers his friends and he keeps in touch with Rich.

When Jesse deals with the public and his teammates, he remembers a golden rule of his childhood: to treat others as he'd like to be treated himself.

In New York, WFAN, an all-sports radio station, hits the air. Waldman leaps at the chance to get into broadcasting. She works the midnight shift, she fills in for vacationing personalities, she covers anything, anytime, anywhere. She has the determination to succeed, just like her first baseball hero, Ted Williams. Her reward is to become the first woman on radio to report on a baseball team full-time.

Baseball is still a man's world, though, and in her first year on the Yankee beat she is covering a game between the Bronx Bombers and the Toronto Blue Jays.

Big George Bell of the Blue Jays hits the game-winning homer and later he is surrounded by reporters at his locker. Suzyn walks over with her microphone. Bell sees her coming and stops talking. He yells at her, saying he won't talk while there is a woman in the locker room. He shouts at her to get out. He refuses to talk again until she is gone.

None of the other reporters stick up for her. The locker room becomes dead quiet. She feels everybody staring at her. Deprived of her right to do her job, she feels angry and ashamed. With tears in her eyes, she turns to leave. Suddenly she hears a voice out of the silence.

"Who's that?" someone wants to know.

"Suzyn Waldman," he is told.

Suzyn Waldman and Jesse Barfield share some laughs outside the Yankee locker room.

The voice pipes up again, this time loud enough for the whole locker room to hear. Loud enough for George Bell to hear.

"Hey, Suzyn, I had three hits today. Do you want to talk to me?" The voice belongs to Jesse Barfield.

Looking back, Suzyn says of Jesse, "What a decent human being. It took a lot of guts to do that, to go against the crowd and stand up for a stranger."

Looking back, Jesse says, "I really respect Suzyn. It was an embarrassing moment for her. I had to do what I thought was right."

One strong woman. One brave man.

Sometimes the paths of good people cross and it can make all the difference in the world.

3

IF AT FIRST...

THE 1906 WHITE SOX AND THE BATTLE FOR CHICAGO

The Cubs owned Chicago.

Sure, the White Sox played here, too. But it was the Cubs who owned this town.

For most of that long season in 1906, the Cubs were the mightiest team in baseball. They could hit and pitch and were on their way to the winningest season in all of baseball history. In a 154 game schedule, the Cubs won 116 times.

Their star pitcher, Three Finger Brown, won twenty-six games.

Defense? They wrote poetry about this infield. Tinkers to Evers to Chance became the most famous double play combination in the history of the game.

Third baseman Harry Steinfeldt, who had given up a career as a traveling minstrel, led the mighty Cub attack with a .327 batting average and led the league in hits and runs batted in.

They were part of the National League, which had been playing professionally since the middle of the 1800s. Now they were the best of the best.

Over on the south side of town the upstart White Sox were floundering. They were part of the expansion American League and had a much smaller core of fans. Those fans would shake their heads

when they saw their White Sox come up to bat. Was there ever a more feeble attack in all of baseball?

They had the lowest team batting average in the league—.230.

They hit only six home runs all year.

Can the big kids on the block be beaten? The Hitless Wonders stage a sixth-inning rally against the mighty Cubs during the 1906 Battle for Chicago.

Only shortstop and captain George Davis gave them any pop with the bat, knocking in eighty runs.

No one wrote poetry about this team but the White Sox did earn a nickname—the "Hitless Wonders."

In early August they were struggling to stay in fourth place. Meanwhile, the Cubs were running away with the National League pennant, winning the flag by twenty games.

But something started happening on the south side of town. The White Sox started winning and didn't stop until they had a nineteen-game winning streak and had climbed into first place over New York and a powerful Cleveland Indians team.

They were a great defensive team and their pitching was strong. They did all the little things a club has to do to win a pennant.

The Windy City couldn't wait for the start of an all-Chicago World Series.

On the West Side of Chicago there was no doubt that the Cubs would win this in a walk. Their fans taunted crosstown White Sox fans, pointing out that their best pitcher was a practicing dentist.

"He's gonna get his teeth knocked out by our guys," Cubs fans yelled. The White Sox rooters heard it all from Cubs fans. What kind of team had a manager who doubled as the left fielder? A guy whose given name at birth was Fielder Jones? "His parents must have known he would be a lousy hitter."

Cubs fans were pretty sure of themselves, and when on the eve of the Series the White Sox's lone hitting star and captain, George Davis, was injured, Cubs fans were all set to start celebrating.

And then game one started. Snow flurries blew across the field. It was bitter cold that October day, but no colder than the White Sox bats.

Five of their first nine hitters struck out. George Rohe, in the lineup only because Davis was injured, could manage only a weak ground ball back to the pitcher.

But White Sox pitcher Nick "Funny Man" Altrock wiped the smiles off the faces of the eager Cubs hitters, allowing just a meager infield hit in four innings. Between the snow, the cold, and the great pitching, it seemed as if no one would get a solid hit all game.

Until the top of the fifth, when substitute Rohe smacked a triple to deep left. One out later, he raced for home on a ball hit back to pitcher Brown. Brown fired to the Cubs catcher, who dropped the ball as Rohe scored the first run of the Series.

Cubs fans gulped. For the first time all season the Cubs looked beatable. The White Sox went on to win the game, 2–1.

Things were back to normal the next day as the Cubs routed the White Sox 7–1, knocking out dentist Doc White in three innings. This was what people expected. If the Cubs could win game three, the White Sox would just fold.

There was no score going into the sixth inning. With no outs, the White Sox loaded the bases on a single, a walk, and a hit batsman. Typical White Sox. Fielder Jones fouled out. The next batter struck out. That left it all up to George Rohe, the substitute, playing only because the team's star was injured. Cubs fans figured to get rid of this scrub in no time.

Instead Rohe tripled to left, clearing the bases. That was all the White Sox needed. They went on to win 3–0 and took a 2–1 lead in the series.

The Cubs came back to win game four but the Sox took game five, scoring eight runs off what was considered the best team in the game. They were just one victory away from the most incredible upset in baseball history.

White Sox fans were delirious. They packed South Side Park. As many as five thousand stood behind a rope in the outfield.

The Cubs were panicking. They sent Three Finger Brown back to the mound on just one day of rest. The White Sox decided to start the pitcher who had nailed down their last victory—the dentist, Doc White. This time, Cub fans were not laughing.

The Cubs jumped out 1–0 but the Sox answered with three runs in the bottom of the first. The third run was scored by none other than the scrub, George Rohe.

In the second inning the Sox scored four more times, chasing Brown from the game. The White Sox won it 8–3. Their fans cheered and cheered and wouldn't stop until the Cubs owner came out on the field and toasted the White Sox as the best team in baseball.

The White Sox owned Chicago.

ONE STUBBORN MOOSE

You're Moose Stubing and they told you to go home. Pack your bags, kid; you're finished.

You couldn't believe it. You were only nineteen. How could they say your baseball days were over?

Just yesterday you were the Bronx high school star belting baseballs over high fences and tall buildings. You were so good the semi-pro New York Mohawks recruited you to play first base. "This guy has muscles on his muscles," your manager boasted. You were his power hitter.

He batted you fourth—clean-up—and he called you Moose.

Thousands cheered your tape-measure shots. Major league scouts heard the noise and they had to see for themselves. "Sign here," said Ed McCarric, top scout for the Pittsburgh Pirates.

He said you still had a lot to learn about baseball. The Pirates sent you to Batavia and the class D minors, the basement of pro ball. The bus rides were long and the food was lousy and you played in crumbling ballparks.

What did you care? You were a lefty slugger going to the big leagues. Or so you thought.

You were still the gentle kid with the man's swing, but now the fastballs were faster. When you finally caught up to the fireballs, the pitchers would snap off a wicked curve. You swung and you missed. You swung and you missed. You swung and you missed.

You're Moose Stubing and they told you to go home.

You didn't break. You took your big swing and your soiled hopes back to the Mohawks. You told yourself you were going to work harder than ever.

The ball started jumping off your bat again. McCarric, the Pirates' scout, saw one of your shots disappear into the deep blue sky. Before it landed, he decided you were worth a second chance. It was on to the minors again. Same bus rides. Same bad food. Same dream. Same curveballs.

They told you to go home again.

When you went back to the Mohawks, even your teammates said it was over. Sure, you had big league power, but you had swung and missed too many times. You had been lucky to get a second chance. The scouts never looked a third time.

A lot of guys fail, Moose. They go home and sulk. They can't even stand to look at a baseball.

You refused to walk away from the game you loved. And in the ashes of your dream, a baseball angel came to take up your cause.

Lou Zaklin, your longtime Mohawk manager, saw you belting the ball again. You asked for his help. He cashed in all his chips on you.

Zaklin telephoned Chick Genovese, a scout for the rival San Francisco Giants. It was a risk for Zaklin, who worked for the Pirates. If Pittsburgh found out about the phone call to Genovese, he could lose his job. But Zaklin, who always admired your talent and your determination, decided you were worth it.

"Hey, Chick," Zaklin asked the Giant scout. "Do me a favor. Come down to the park this afternoon and see this Stubing kid."

"What, are you kidding?" asked Genovese. "The guy's been cut twice already. He's a waste of time."

"Chick, have you ever wasted an afternoon of your life before?" Zaklin pleaded. "Come on. I'll pay your cab fare."

You didn't hit a home run that day, Moose. You didn't even get a base hit. But you crushed two long foul balls. You hit them so hard that Chick Genovese signed you to a Giants contract.

You played minor league ball for ten years. You drifted from team to team, always working hard, always learning a little bit more about baseball. You had some big years and you always had the respect of your teammates.

You grew old in the minor leagues. Your bat slowed down. You were fading, Moose Stubing. It looked like your dream was dying.

Suddenly, you were an Angel.

In the blink of an eye you were called up to the big leagues, a late-season pickup for the California Angels. You had made it to the majors.

What would the gods of baseball like to say about you, Larry Moose Stubing? That you won a pennant for your team, that you powered major league fastballs into the cheering center field bleachers, that you went on to an unforgettable career?

It didn't happen like that. Five times you got up to bat for the Angels in that September of 1967. Four times you struck out. You never got a big league hit.

That hurt.

You thought about hanging up your spikes and going home. Only, Moose Stubing doesn't quit. You finished out your playing career in the minors. The Angel organization was impressed with your baseball knowledge and your love of the game. They asked you to stay on as a minor league manager.

You began passing on your determination and your work habits to young players. You did it so well, the Angels wanted you in their major league clubhouse. They asked you to be their third-base coach, an incredible accomplishment for a guy they said was finished with pro baseball thirty years before.

You loved every minute of your job. The players you admired most were the ones who kept on trying. On your team was a pitcher by the name of Jim Abbott, who has only one hand. The experts tried to tell him to forget it, too.

After a lifetime in pro ball, you root for every player—from little leaguers to big leaguers—who won't quit. Who can blame you?

You're Moose Stubing and they told you to go home.

LOYALTY'S REWARD: GIL HODGES AND TOMMIE AGEE

In the city streets of Brooklyn, they loved a strong and gentle country boy from Indiana named Gil Hodges. He played a great first base for the Brooklyn Dodgers and he smashed balls out of Ebbets Field.

The fans saw more than that in him. A streak of decency ran through Hodges as long as Flatbush Avenue. He'd break up fights on the field with a reasoned word or a powerful stare. The bigots who slung their vile remarks toward teammate Jackie Robinson would shut their mouths when Hodges was around. The slugger was patient and obliging to any kid who stopped to ask for his autograph.

Brooklyn was more than a place where he earned his living. The country boy made it his home. He married a Brooklyn girl. They bought a home there and together they went to a neighborhood church every Sunday.

On the field Hodges helped answer the prayers of Brooklyn fans by leading the Dodgers to a pennant in 1952. He was a clutch hitter, the guy you could count on, driving in 102 runs and clubbing 32 homers to lead the team. The patient Hodges even drew an incredible 107 walks. (It's always astonishing when a power hitter walks more than he strikes out.)

Maybe this would be the year the boys from Brooklyn would finally win a World Series. They'd have to beat the hated Yankees to do it,

Hodges hangs out with Brooklyn kids before a ballgame.

but the fans believed that with the mighty Hodges on their side, they'd have a chance.

The eyes of Brooklyn looked to Hodges as the Series began. In the first game, he went 0-for-3. Then 0-for-3 again. All year long, he'd been knocking runners in. Now he was letting them die on base. Game three was another 0-for-3 for Hodges. In games four and five their hero was hitless again.

After his hitless World Series, Gil Hodges wanted to assure his loyal fans that he, too, was keeping the faith. Here he warms up his bats on a cold winter afternoon at Coney Island.

In some other town, some other player would have been buried with boos and catcalls. Not in Brooklyn. Not Gil Hodges.

Every time he came up to bat, the cheers grew louder. During Sunday church services across Brooklyn, prayers were said for the Dodgers' first baseman.

In game six he couldn't buy a hit. And in game seven, when the Dodgers really needed him to deliver, Hodges went 0-for-4, as Brooklyn lost the World Series.

Twenty-one times up. Twenty-one times down. Not a single hit for Hodges.

A player could crumble after a performance like that. But Brooklyn fans never lost patience with Hodges. The next season they cheered him on, certain that he would start smacking the ball again. Their cheers meant a lot to Hodges. If the fans could be patient with him, he could be patient with himself.

That year Hodges rewarded them with his best season ever, batting .302 and driving in 122 runners. And even though the Dodgers lost the 1953 Series, Hodges was Brooklyn's hitting star.

Two years later he led the Dodgers to their first championship, as Brooklyn beat the Yankees 2–0 in the deciding Series game. Hodges knocked in both runners.

In 1957 Brooklyn lost their first baseman and their team when the Dodgers moved to Los Angeles. For five years New York didn't have a National League team to root for. Then, in 1962, the Mets were born, and Brooklyn Dodgers fans were there to cheer them on.

The Mets were horrible. Their first year they set an all-time record for most losses ever in a season—120. The country called them the Lovable Losers. Their pitchers couldn't pitch. Their hitters couldn't hit.

They finished sixty and a half games out of first place. Their winningest pitcher lost twenty-four games. They had a catcher named Choo Choo and two pitchers named Bob Miller. Choo Choo couldn't hit and, together, the Millers could manage just three wins against fourteen losses.

On the last play of the season, the Mets hit into a triple play.

The Mets stayed bad. Players came and went as managers just lost patience with their ragged play. The Mets owners had to do something. They needed a man to guide their young players, a man with strength and loyalty and patience, someone who commanded respect and who could help the young players along.

They chose Gil Hodges.

In his first year, 1968, the Mets weren't much better. They kept losing. Hodges looked at his team. He saw his young players making mistakes, sometimes failing miserably. One of those players was Tommie Agee, a young outfielder the Mets had acquired from the Chicago White Sox.

Agee bobbled balls in the outfield and he was overmatched at the plate. In only 368 at bats, he struck out 103 times. Still, there was something Hodges saw in Agee. Even if he hit a simple one-hopper to the pitcher, he ran it out hard. He was always trying his best.

So Hodges kept sending Agee out there, telling him not to give up. Hodges began to believe in Agee and the young Mets, and although they finished the season ninth in a ten-team division, they began to believe in themselves.

You can call what happened the next year a miracle. Everyone does. Led by Hodges, the lowly Mets, with their collection of young players and over-the-hill veterans, began to win ball games. The same losing pitching staff that Hodges wouldn't give up on turned it around—guys like Tom Seaver and Jerry Koosman and Nolan Ryan.

And Hodges kept playing Agee. His patience paid off. Agee blossomed into a pretty sensational outfielder. And at the plate, last year's strikeout king showed patience and confidence, leading the team in runs batted in.

By September the Mets overtook the first-place Chicago Cubs. On September 24, 1969, the amazing happened: They clinched their division championship. Later they swept the Atlanta Braves for the pennant.

They went to the World Series and ran smack into the Baltimore

Orioles, a team everyone called the greatest in baseball. Even a lot of Mets fans were ready to concede after the Orioles won the first game of the Series.

But Gil Hodges wasn't ready to push the panic button. He told his team to just go out and keep trying. The Mets came back and won four straight. There was great pitching by Koosman and Seaver and clutch hitting by Donn Clendenon and little-known Al Weis.

But what everyone talked about most were the two catches made in center field by Agee. In the fourth inning of the third game, with the Series tied at a game apiece, the Orioles threatened with men on first and third. Elrod Hendricks powered a ball to deep left center field. To the fans it looked like two runs were certain. But Agee refused to give up on the ball.

At the last second he reached across his body and made a back-

Miracles of miracles: Agee snares a sinking line drive in the 1969 World Series as teammate Art Shamsky watches in amazement.

handed stab. End of the inning. End of the threat. The Orioles were deflated.

In the seventh inning, the Orioles had one last gasp. They loaded the bases. With two out, young fireballer Nolan Ryan came in to pitch. Oriole Paul Blair greeted him with a screaming line drive to center. Three runs were as good as on the scoreboard.

Out of nowhere came Agee. He dove and slid on his belly, snaring the sinking line drive. The Orioles were crushed. The Mets went on to win the game and the Series.

People still call it a miracle. Ask the Mets players, though, and they'll tell you different. To a man, they say they won because of the lessons they learned about patience and strength and determination. Lessons learned a generation earlier and passed on to them by a decent man named Gil Hodges.

4

HARD TIMES

NO QUIT SCHMIDT

"Twenty years ago I came here as a country boy from Ohio to . . ."

Pencils scribbled. Cameras clicked. Videotape rolled. The powerful ballplayer's broken voice stunned the room. Tough guy Mike Schmidt, the owner of 548 career home runs, began to cry. Not just a few tears, but a raging river.

What makes a person cry?

Sometimes it's pain. Sometimes it's joy. And sometimes, as in Mike Schmidt's case, it's something else.

Growing up, Mike's best sports were football and basketball. But by the time he graduated from high school he had ripped up both knees. Those injuries might just have been a blessing in disguise. They forced him to concentrate on baseball. Schmidt already had a rocket arm and lightning reflexes. If he could only learn to hit the curveball he'd be a good ballplayer.

Only he looked so silly trying to hit the curve no one expected Schmidt ever to earn his living playing baseball. But they couldn't see inside of him. They couldn't know how badly he wanted to succeed.

His high school coach caught glimpses of Mike's desire. During batting practice he didn't want the pitchers throwing the easy fastballs. He wanted the pitcher to break off his best curve, the pitch that gave Schmidt the most trouble. Very few young ball players have the guts to work on their weaknesses. Very few have the guts to work so hard at something that does not come so easily. But nothing would stop Schmidt. After a heavy snowfall in April, Schmidt rounded up his teammates. He called up his coach, who assumed everyone would know practice had been canceled because of the weather.

"Where are you?" Schmidt asked his coach. The coach had to hand it to Schmidt. The kid had desire.

Still, the colleges weren't knocking his door down when it came time to hand out athletic scholarships. Schmidt enrolled at Ohio University, partly because a high school teammate was going there, partly because of his desire to be an architect.

His hard work began to pay off. He caught the interest of a Philadelphia Phillies scout, who saw in Schmidt a touch of talent, a bit of power, and a wonderful work ethic. Schmidt was signed to a minor league contract.

Now the curveballs coming at him were thrown by professionals. He had a lousy year. He hit only .211. That only made him work harder. And the next year he played so well the Phillies brought him up to the major leagues for the last month of the 1972 season.

Schmidt got his first look at a major league curveball.

He couldn't get near it.

He struck out nearly half the time he stepped into the batter's box. The next year was just as much of a struggle. He hit .196 and when the fans weren't booing they were wondering why the Phillies were making this kid the third baseman of the future.

He kept working through the boos and the strikeouts. After his disastrous rookie season he refused to go home and mope. Instead, he went to Puerto Rico to play winter ball and he vowed he would learn how to hit that curveball.

When the 1974 season opened Schmidt was ready. A lot of pitchers who figured to make Schmidt look silly on a curveball were surprised to see him launching the pitches four hundred feet over outfield walls. He hit thirty-six homers that season and emerged as one of the best fielding third basemen in the league.

Over the next few years, Schmidt learned to cut down on his strikeouts. He learned to walk more. He became a reliable hitter with men on base. He became a regular at the All Star game. The Gold Glove Award, given to the best fielder at each position, went to Schmidt ten times. He earned a reputation as the hardest working player in the league. His coaches marveled at how prepared he was for every game.

He led his team to the World Championship in 1980, the first of back-to-back years he was voted as the National League's MVP. When all was said and done, the guy who was nothing special in high school had become the best all-around third baseman in the history of the game.

"I never knew I was going to be that good," Schmidt said. No one else did either. You never know what can come from hard work and believing in yourself.

On May 28, 1989, in the ninth inning of a Sunday afternoon game, Schmidt drew a walk and trotted down to first base. He said to his first base coach, "That's it, I'll never play another game." After eighteen seasons, Schmidt knew his career was at an end. No matter how hard he worked, now it wasn't enough. It was time to call it quits and he called a press conference to announce his decision.

Schmidt sat in front of writers and television cameras as he thought back on his career, all he had done, and the hard work it took to do it. All the missed curveballs, all the ground balls. The strikeouts. The homers. The boos and the cheers. Practicing in the snow. The knowledge that if he hadn't mustered the courage to work on his weaknesses, he would never have been so great.

It was all too much to keep in. He cried out loud.

Mike Schmidt didn't let early failures stop him. He wipes a tear from his eye as he announces his retirement after a glorious career.

Part of it was a sadness at saying good-bye. Part of it was just a man realizing how hard he had toiled. It was a release after trying so hard and so long and seeing how far he had come.

These were tears of accomplishment.

Mike Schmidt never took the easy way out. He left the game the way he came in: taking his cuts; giving his all; unafraid.

A LEGEND NAMED LOU

The boy looked at the big red ball rising in the sky and pumped his fist in the air. All right, Ben thought to himself, it's a sunny day. What a perfect morning to visit Uncle Lou.

Ben had spent special Saturdays with his great-uncle, Lou Zaklin, ever since he was a little boy.

One time he and Uncle Lou rode the subway to Yankee Stadium. He never forgot that day. The Yanks had lost in the last inning. Ben started crying. Uncle Lou had gathered Ben in his arms and given him a big hug.

That was seasons ago. Ben wondered what Uncle Lou would have planned today as his mother drove toward the Bronx. Maybe they'd play a game of "flies up," he decided, as he rang Uncle Lou's doorbell. "I'll pick you up after work," said Mom.

While feasting on his uncle's blueberry pancakes, Ben couldn't contain himself any longer. He asked where they would be going.

"We're going to a church," said Uncle Lou.

Church? Ben thought to himself. On such a great baseball day?

"Oh, okay," Ben said, smiling weakly, trying to hide his disappointment.

They walked for fifteen minutes on sunbaked sidewalks, past the firehouse, past a playground. When they walked by a ball field, Ben

Lou Gehrig joins in a neighborhood game of hardball.

looked longingly at a kid flying around the bases. Finally he and Uncle Lou crossed Riverdale Avenue and came to Christ Episcopal Church.

They walked inside. The church was old and beautiful. The sun was shining through stained glass windows.

As Ben and Uncle Lou walked around the empty sanctuary, Ben could hear their own footsteps.

They approached the altar. Suddenly Ben saw a nameplate on the altar rail.

"Look, Uncle Lou. It says Lou Gehrig. Is this the same Lou Gehrig who once played for the Yanks?"

Uncle Lou nodded and smiled.

"Did you ever see him play?"

"Sure did."

"Was he any good?" asked Ben. "How many homers did he hit?"

"Sit down, Son," said Uncle Lou, pointing to a bench in front of the Lou Gehrig nameplate. "You can judge ball players by statistics, I guess. Lou Gehrig ranks with the best of them there. He hit 493 homers, 23 grand slams, drove in nearly 2,000 runs."

"Wow!" said Ben.

"Yeah, that's something," said Uncle Lou, "but that's not how I remember Lou Gehrig.

"I used to go out to the stadium as a kid and watch him play. He was so strong, it looked like the baseball would break in half when he hit it. Year after year, Gehrig would be banging out homers, driving in runs. He batted right behind Babe Ruth in the lineup. Everyone would make a big fuss out of the Babe, but Lou Gehrig was my guy.

"He was a real gentleman, soft-spoken and kind. He never walked away from a kid who wanted his autograph. He was a part of my life. I thought he'd be playing forever. Fact is, he set a record for playing in 2,130 consecutive games. Iron Lou, they called him, because he seemed indestructible."

Ben looked at him puzzled.

"Indestructible," said Uncle Lou. "Something that can't be broken.

"Then one day in 1939, I heard Lou Gehrig wasn't in the lineup. It was the first game he missed in fifteen years. It seems Lou was sick. Not the kind of stomachache sick where you feel better in a few days, but real serious. The muscles in his body were falling apart. I looked in the paper every day for good news about Lou, but there wasn't any. Doctors said it was a mystery ailment. They didn't know when Lou would feel better.

"He never did play baseball again. A few months later, on July Fourth, he was back at Yankee Stadium to say good-bye.

"I was supposed to play in a ball game that day, but I told the guys I couldn't make it. I had to go see Lou.

"There were 70,000 of us in the stands that day. We all knew he was pretty sick.

"Some of Lou's old teammates were there. Gehrig looked terrible. He was stooped over, like he could barely stand. I remember a guy saying over the loudspeaker, 'Lou has asked me to thank all of you. He is too moved to speak.' Everyone started chanting, 'We want Gehrig! We want Gehrig!' Then he walked up to the microphone. You could hear a pin drop."

"What did he say?" Ben asked.

"I'll never forget it for as long as I live. Lou Gehrig said he was the luckiest man on the face of the earth."

"Lucky?"

"Yep. He said he had been lucky to play with a great bunch of guys. He said he had a mother and father who worked all their lives so that he could have an education and a strong body. He said when you have a wife who is a tower of strength and courage it's a blessing. Ben, I'll never forget his final words: 'I might have had a bad break, but I have an awful lot to live for.'

"Grown men were crying. I was choked up myself. My hero had come through. But there's something not many people know. They say the measure of a man is how he reacts to hard times. Well, Lou Gehrig never quit on life.

"He got a job counseling boys in trouble. As sick as he was, he went to work every day. One time he walked into work on crutches. He was sweating with fever and he had trouble breathing. He sat across from a tough young punk named Rocco Barbella, who wanted

Uncle Lou passes down the Gehrig legend to Ben in Gehrig's old church.

A LEGEND NAMED LOU □ 95

to get out of reform school. Gehrig told the boy he had caused his mother a lot of grief, that he wasn't fit to be out on the streets. He sent him back to reform school for another year.

"At first, Barbella was mad. But he went back to reform school and straightened himself out. A couple of years later he changed his name to Rocky Graziano and became boxing's middleweight champion of the world. He wanted to go shake Gehrig's hand.

"But he couldn't. Lou Gehrig was dead.

"He had passed away in his home, a block from this church. They held the funeral right here in this room. Thousands of his fans showed up. The line into the church was four blocks long.

"In the Hall of Fame, there is a plaque that tells all about Lou Gehrig as a ball player. They put this nameplate here in this church to remember a good man.

"We all have our ways of remembering him. I changed my name to Lou from Louis. Had it done legally and everything. Then I found out Lou Gehrig's proper name was really Louis."

Uncle Lou let out a chuckle. "And now, here I am telling you about him so you can pass it on."

Uncle Lou was smiling but Ben thought he had a tear in his eye. The boy gave his uncle a hug.

"C'mon, boy," said Uncle Lou. "We better be going."

They walked out across Riverdale Avenue. Five minutes later, they were standing in a park. Uncle Lou took a red rubber ball out of his jacket pocket. "Hey, Ben, think fast." Uncle Lou threw a high pop-up. Ben circled under it. He tripped and tumbled over a loose tree branch. "Are you okay?" Uncle Lou asked.

"Sure," said the boy. "I'm Iron Ben."

Uncle Lou laughed. They played ball well past lunchtime, with Ben fielding grounders Uncle Lou threw. It was sometime during their walk home that Ben decided he was the luckiest boy on the face of the earth.

ALL EYES ON EISENREICH

The pitch came in. The batter swung.

Crack.

The baseball went screaming up the right field alley. He hit it so hard it looked as if the ball might not have time to climb out of the park. But the right fielder watched the line drive clear the fence and sail into the vast Midwest night.

A game-winning home run for Jim Eisenreich.

The Kansas City Royals fans roared as he rounded the bases. They chanted his name. When he reached home plate, his teammates welcomed him with back slaps and high fives.

Jim Eisenreich let himself smile. For the Kansas City hero, the game-winning home run was better than just a romp around the bases.

There was a time when Eisenreich was afraid to play on a baseball field. His troubles began when he was eight. Jim was a good ball player. But sometimes while he was playing, his body would start twitching. His neck jerked and his arms thrashed wildly. His eyes, nose, and mouth twisted into the funniest faces.

But there was nothing funny about it to Jim. He was terrified. These fits came out of nowhere. He couldn't help them.

His mom and dad took him to the doctor. They couldn't figure out what was wrong. Jim kept on playing. He loved baseball and he was great at it. Playing ball was all he ever wanted to do. Nothing was going to stop him.

As strange as Jim's twitching tics were, his friends grew used to them. His teammates in high school and college always supported him. No one was surprised when, just out of college, he was signed to a minor league contract by the Minnesota Twins. It didn't take long before Jim was a rookie center fielder for the Twins. Early on he looked like a good bet to win the 1982 Rookie of the Year award.

His lifelong dream of being a big league star was coming true.

It was April 30, 1982, the sixth inning of a game against the Milwaukee Brewers. Inside the Metrodome, Eisenreich was like a boy in a bubble, playing center field with 23,547 pairs of eyes trained on him.

He started to twitch—more than normal. He was shaking and he went into convulsions. He had trouble breathing, was gasping for air and felt like he was trapped in a small closet. He raced off the field and escaped into the dugout. He shook it off but the same thing happened the next night. And the night after. He didn't know what was happening. He wanted so badly to believe it would get better.

It only got worse.

By now the whole country had heard about this "strange" outfielder for the Twins. And when Minnesota came into Boston for a three-game series against the Red Sox, some fans were waiting for Eisenreich.

He took his place in center field in Fenway Park, a tiny ballpark where the fans sit right on top of the field. Some of them yelled at Eisenreich, "Shake. Shake. Shake." They wanted to make the game difficult for him.

In the second inning, Eisenreich did start shaking. He had to take himself out of the game. The fans howled with laughter.

It happened again a few days later in Milwaukee. He left the game again. This couldn't go on. The Twins decided his season was over and sent him to several doctors.

Eisenreich was crushed. All he had ever wanted to do was play major league baseball and now, because of some strange ailment, he couldn't.

One doctor said it was stage fright. Eisenreich said no, it wasn't nervousness he felt. Another doctor said he had a fear of open spaces. Eisenreich couldn't buy that either. No boy from the rolling plains of the Midwest is frightened of open spaces.

He tried a number of comebacks but they all failed. For five years he was out of baseball, living with his parents, bouncing from doctor to doctor in search of answers.

Finally he accepted the diagnosis of some doctors who said he was suffering from a rare condition called Tourette's Syndrome. This was not an emotional problem. It was a physical one. The tics and twitches could be controlled with medicine.

Everyone felt relieved. Finally there was an explanation. Now Eisenreich faced another challenge. He wanted to get back into the major leagues. It wouldn't be easy—the Twins had already given up on him. Would anyone give him another chance?

As luck would have it, there was someone who remembered Eisenreich from his childhood. Bob Hegman had played ball with Eisenreich in college. Now he was working for the Kansas City Royals. He took a chance on a friend.

Jim Eisenreich made it back, all right. You can look up his 1989 statistics, his best year. He was extremely popular with his teammates. They voted him player of the year, ahead of Bo Jackson. The fans loved him.

Sweetest of all, he played the outfield with the greatest of ease.

A ballpark full of fans would watch him: Jim Eisenreich, hands on knees, crouched, fixed, focused. His mind alert, his body still as the night. Ready.

ROGER MARIS: ALONE IN A CROWD

They say everything has a season. A time to celebrate and a time to despair.

But Roger Maris's summer of glory was also his season of struggle. The good and the bad collided for Maris in one explosive year.

That memorable season of 1961 came as a surprise to everyone, most of all to Maris. He was a quiet ball player from North Dakota with a prairie man's lonesome pride. As a teenager, working on the railroad, he was taught to do a job till it was done right. He respected others and expected others to treat him with dignity. When he married his high school sweetheart, it was forever. He was proud of his children and spent every chance he could with them.

He had to be away a lot because his job was to play right field for the New York Yankees. He kissed his family good-bye before the start of the 1961 season. And when his wife, Pat, became very ill carrying their fourth child, Maris took this pain with him as he traveled from ballpark to ballpark belting home runs.

You could always spot Roger Maris on a ballfield. He was the guy wearing a boy's crew cut, his powerful biceps rippling under the high cut-off sleeves of his Yankee uniform.

When he hit a home run, he rounded the bases head down, running quickly, eager to touch home, as if he might melt under the flame

Roger Maris was happiest when he was with his family.

of adoration. He'd cross the plate and shake the hand of his best buddy, Mickey Mantle. Then he would slip into the dugout and disappear.

Maris and Mantle both hit so many homers in the late spring of '61, fans thought either one had a chance to break the untouchable single-season record of sixty set by Babe Ruth.

Before the first day of summer, Maris had already collected twenty-five home runs. Mantle kept pace with him. The fans called Mantle and Maris the M and M boys.

This should have been a great time for Maris. But strange things began to happen. He'd come up to bat and half the crowd would be booing. Even lots of hometown fans wanted him to fail. He knew what it was all about.

Ruth was baseball's all-time hero. They called Yankee Stadium the House that Ruth Built. The ghost of The Babe made Maris feel he was playing in a haunted house. How dare he even challenge the Babe's sacred record, many fans believed. They felt he had no right.

If anyone was going to break the Bambino's hallowed mark, let it be the Mick, the fans said. Mantle had been a Bronx Bomber for ten years, a genuine Yankee hero with a Ruthian swing.

Maris was treated like an upstart. He had just come to the team the year before and fans thought he was stealing Mantle's thunder.

What fans didn't know was that Mantle and Maris were actually good friends. They cheered for each other at the ballpark and after the game they went home together to the apartment they shared.

The summer wore on and Maris kept doing great things. The boos just got louder. Even the lords of baseball turned against him.

The commissioner, Ford Frick, ruled that Maris had to break the record in 154 games, the length of the season in Ruth's day. If not, Maris's achievement would go into the record books stained with an asterisk.

Strange—no other record in baseball was protected that way.

Sportswriters began to hound Maris in the clubhouse. They wanted a happy, outgoing hero who loved the publicity. But Maris was painfully shy, and every spare thought was tied up in worry about his sick wife.

Maris was in no mood to go out partying with sportswriters and New York celebrities. He just wanted to go home. Some people thought he was unfriendly. A few reporters turned on Maris. They wrote stories about how much they disliked Maris, how surly he was, how all he cared about was hitting home runs.

The people who really knew him couldn't believe it. His fellow Yankees knew Maris as a real team player. He defended right field as hard as he swung the bat. He'd bunt a guy home if that's what it took to score a run.

Back home, Roger's wife heard the mean things being said about him. How could people say her husband had a bad temper, she wondered? He wasn't like that at home. Roger was as kind as the day was long.

Maris suffered the insults in silence but inside he was churning. When his hair started falling out, doctors said it was because of the terrible pressure he was under. The only peace Maris found was on the ball field. He kept hitting home runs, getting closer and closer to Ruth's record.

It reminded Maris of when he was playing high school football back in Fargo, North Dakota. In his town there were two high schools and they were bitter rivals. When Maris led his football team to victory over its archenemy, half the town hated him. He couldn't understand why. It was supposed to be just a game. And now this season of baseball was just like that year in high school—not much fun at all.

Late in the summer Maris fell into a miserable hitting slump. He had forty-nine homers but he went through a stretch where he managed just one hit in eighteen at bats. It was the low point of his season.

Then one day after a game he was given a message: His wife had given birth to a boy. Mother and child were doing well. On his next day off he flew home to spend time with the family. He cradled Randy, his newborn son, and he knew this was more important than any home run.

Even back on the ball field Maris had more important things to consider than Ruth's record. On September 1 the second-place Tigers were in New York for a crucial series against the first-place Yanks. Detroit was just one game back in the standings.

More than anything, Maris wanted to help his team win. He made great plays in the field and belted two home runs in one game.

The Yanks swept the Tigers and suddenly the pennant race was all but over. A couple of weeks later Mantle's season was all but over, too. An injury forced him out of the lineup and he fell out of the home run chase.

The focus now was entirely on Maris. The press and the fans watched his every move. He was closing in on the record. Some fans were still hoping he would fail.

The injured Mantle tried to rally everybody behind his buddy. "I'm rooting for him," said Mantle. "Let's everybody root for him."

After 153 games, Maris had 58 home runs. Nine games remained in the season, but baseball commissioner Ford Frick said Maris had only one game left to catch the Babe. That meant Maris had to hit two home runs to tie Ruth.

His chances were slim. The Yanks were playing a night game in Baltimore, Ruth's hometown. This was also the only ballpark in which Maris had failed to hit a home run that season.

When he came to bat for the first time, the crowd became quiet. Maris got good wood on the ball. He smacked a vicious shot but didn't hit it high enough. The line drive was caught for an out.

In the third inning, Oriole pitcher Milt Pappas challenged Maris with another fastball. Roger swung. The ball rocketed deep to right field. The crowd roared. Home run number fifty-nine.

Maris's pursuit of Ruth was still alive. He was one shy of the record when he came up to bat in the fourth. The Baltimore crowd was roaring, almost unbelievably, pulling for Maris. They felt like they were a part of history. The Orioles' new pitcher, Dick Hall, delivered

The loneliness of the long distance hitter: Broadcaster Phil Rizzuto (right) tries to comfort Maris as the pressure of the home run chase mounts.

and Maris connected. Deep to right. The fans rose to their feet screaming. But Maris knew right away.

It was a foul ball. Then, trying too hard, Maris chased a high fastball and struck out. Never before had he felt so much pressure playing in a game.

In the seventh inning, Maris again hit a long foul ball. Then he really got hold of one. The ball soared high in the sky and deep. The right fielder raced back to the wall. At the last moment the ball died and settled in the outfielder's glove.

Maris came to bat one last time in the ninth. Hoyt Wilhelm came in to pitch. Wilhelm threw his famous knuckleball, a pitch that danced slowly toward home plate, then swerved at the last moment. No one, not even Wilhelm, knew where it was going. Hitting that knuckleball was like trying to catch a butterfly. Maris lunged at the pitch but tapped it meekly back to Wilhelm.

Back in the clubhouse, the writers crowded around Maris. They expected to find him growling or throwing a temper tantrum. They were wrong. Maris felt relieved. He had given it his best shot and had come up a little short. Or so Commissioner Frick had said.

But Maris had a legion of young fans who cheered him on. The season wasn't over for them; Maris still had eight games left. They figured if Maris broke Ruth's record by the end of the season, he would be the new home run king. No commissioner could change that.

When the Yanks returned home, even old die-hard New York fans had begun to appreciate what Maris had achieved. Now that the ghost of Ruth had disappeared, they began pulling for Rog.

The best news for the Yankee slugger was that his wife arrived in New York for those last five games at Yankee Stadium.

In the first game back against the Orioles, Maris swung at a high curveball and watched the ball rise and rise until it bounced off the facade of the upper deck. He had done it. He had tied Babe Ruth. Home run number sixty.

Rounding the bases, Maris felt as if a great weight had been lifted. After the game, Babe Ruth's widow came over to congratulate him. At last Maris welled up with emotion. He told her, "I'm glad I didn't break the Babe's record in 154 games. This record is enough for me."

Maris didn't hit another home run over the next three games. It all came down to the final game of the season, a matinee against the Boston Red Sox.

Maris came up with two out in the fourth inning. There was no score. Tracy Stallard's first two pitches missed the plate. The crowd booed. Maris deserved something decent to swing at.

The booing lit Stallard's competitive fire. He put everything he had into his next delivery.

Maris swung. Time seemed to stop. Maris looked up and followed the flight of the ball. The crowd stood as one, their heads turned to right field. In the radio booth, broadcaster Phil Rizzuto shouted into his microphone, "This could be it. . . . There it goes. Number sixty-one."

Roger Maris had done it. He had hit more home runs than any other man in a single season.

Maris was offered the opportunity to make extra money by going on a whirlwind exhibition tour. He said no. "I have a wife and children," he said. "I have been away all summer and I don't intend to be away all winter."

Roger Maris played ball for seven more years. He remained a private man who loved baseball but loved his family more. Over time, the world began to see that his shyness wasn't arrogance, that his honesty wasn't rudeness. He was simply a man who wanted to do a job until it was done right and then go home to his wife and children.

Over the years Yankee fans wanted to show Maris they had been wrong about him. But Maris's pride kept him away from Yankee Stadium. He believed the writers and the Yankee organization had given him a bum rap. Eventually, the writers and the fans and even the Yankees agreed. Maris deserved better.

In 1984, the Yankees invited Maris back for a special day in his honor. This time he accepted. More than fifty thousand people packed Yankee Stadium to welcome Maris home, and when he was introduced, the fans erupted in cheers. His buddy, Mickey Mantle, was there once again to shake his hand. His wife was at his side.

The crowd cheered louder than they had ever cheered any of his home runs. Maris let himself bathe in the applause.

At that moment it didn't matter to him that he was sick with cancer.

For Roger Maris and baseball, this was a time to heal.

5

THE JOY OF
THE GAME

ERNIE BANKS: "LET'S PLAY TWO"

He was the oldest boy, so it was his job to chase away the rats. He lugged in the drinking water from the outside pump and gathered the firewood. By the age of ten, he was off picking cotton with his father. His dad worked seven days a week but the family was still poor. Some days the boy missed lunch; some nights he had to go to bed hungry.

Christmas? That was just another day off from school. There were no presents and no tree. Sometimes he would stand outside the grocery store to wait for the food the store would throw away.

This is a portrait of a happy boy named Ernie Banks.

Maybe Ernie's family didn't have much money, but they shared what little they had. And when it came to love and hugs, there was always plenty to go around. On winter nights they'd gather around the wood stove and read. Some nights the stove got so red-hot it threatened to set the house on fire. Ernie's father and mother would stand guard on either side of the stove while the kids did their homework.

Picking cotton was back-breaking work for a young boy. He had to crawl on his hands and knees all day alongside his father in the hot sun. But Ernie always looked forward to those moments before the workday started, when his dad took him to the local coffee shop and they shared a sweet roll.

Ernie felt lucky. He measured his life not by what he couldn't have, but by what he could. That's how he fell in love with sports.

He lived eight blocks from a YMCA. The men who ran it were kind and they let kids play ball there for free. Ernie started playing basketball. When he was in high school he was able to take up softball for the first time.

He was a natural. He had quick wrists that swung a bat like a whip. Even the older players from the area's best fast-pitch softball league had to check him out. They liked what they saw and overnight he became their shortstop.

Someone else was watching him, too. Bill Blair, a player and scout for the Colts, a Negro League baseball team, offered seventeen-year-old Ernie Banks a tryout. He packed his bags for Amarillo, Texas, leaving home for the very first time.

It was a long, dusty drive over 319 miles of tough Texas turf. He tried to pass the time by sleeping but he was too nervous.

Ernie wasn't allowed to stay in a hotel where white people stayed. So he ended up in an old hotel for blacks only, with tired furniture and peeling walls. He was just glad to have a bed and he got ready for a good night's sleep. That's when his roommate told him to look up at the ceiling. Ernie saw a hole in the roof big enough to see the sky. Water dripped in, soaking the floor.

Some guys might have complained. Not Ernie Banks, who always looked on the bright side of everything. "They must think we're two new stars," he said to his roommate, "because they gave us the starlight room."

Making the team was a cinch for Ernie. He played all summer for the Colts and at the end, they paid him $12.50. He came home excited, putting every penny on the kitchen table for his family.

The next summer a baseball legend named Cool Papa Bell saw

Ernie play. He was so impressed with Ernie, he told his friends with the Kansas City Monarchs to sign him. It wasn't long before Ernie was playing shortstop for the Monarchs, the top team in all the Negro Leagues.

Ernie was a star there, too. He loved every minute of every game. His greatness seemed to spring from his joy. He loved the sweet smell of a ball field after a gentle summer rain, the mudleather feel of his glove scooping up a grounder. He savored the sounds of the game, the crack of the bat, the infield chatter, and the pop of a fastball in the catcher's mitt.

Another sound Ernie Banks heard a lot was the crowd roaring at another of his big blasts. Major league scouts heard that sound, too, and in 1953 Ernie was signed by the Chicago Cubs. He was so talented that he skipped playing in the minors and rocketed straight to the big leagues.

This was just as he had hoped it would be the night he saw the stars through the hole in his hotel room ceiling. Ernie Banks was a shining star.

He gobbled up ground balls at shortstop and he destroyed major league pitching. Belting more than forty home runs a season, he quickly became one of baseball's most feared power hitters.

He won back-to-back MVP awards, baseball's highest honor, in 1958 and 1959. But his Cubs were a terrible team. They never came close to winning a pennant, usually finishing toward the bottom of the National League standings.

Sometimes great ball players on bad teams complain. They say they deserve to play on a winning team and often demand to be traded to a pennant contender. Not Ernie Banks. He was loyal to his team and devoted to his fans.

One time he went on an overnight fishing trip with a couple of buddies. Soon all the kids in town heard that a great baseball hero was visiting. They found out where he was staying. The next morn-

Ernie Banks shared his joy of the game all year long. During the Christmas season he has a field day with his young fans.

ing, three hundred bicycles stood outside the house. One of Ernie's pals suggested he sneak out the back so none of the kids would bother him.

"Naw, we can't do that to them," Banks said.

He walked out on the front porch and shook hands with every

single kid. He signed an autograph for each of them. And when it was finally time to leave, the happy kids escorted him down the street on their bicycles, waving to their hero.

Ernie always seemed to be in a good mood, always ready to sign an autograph or play another game. Some days in August it would get so hot in Chicago that the heat from the sun would beat off the old brick wall surrounding Wrigley Field. Everyone at the ballpark seemed lifeless. Then Ernie Banks would pop out of the dugout, look around, and say, "What a beautiful day for baseball. Let's play two."

If they did, the Cubs would likely end up losing both games. For sixteen seasons it went like this: Banks played great, the Cubs played terrible. And then, in 1969, the Cubs were in first place for most of the summer. It looked as if Ernie was finally going to get to live out his dream of playing in a World Series. He was driving in runs and playing spectacularly in the field.

But in the last month of the season, the Cubs fell apart. The upstart New York Mets were putting together a miracle season. For Ernie Banks, it was a nightmare. The Mets overtook the Cubs and, on the day the Cubs lost the pennant race, Ernie Banks was crushed. He wouldn't get to play in a World Series after all.

On his way home from the ballpark he stopped his car along the waterfront on Lake Michigan and he cried.

The next year Ernie Banks was back at old Wrigley Field. He was full of smiles and rarin' to go. Banks was almost forty years old but he still played with the joy of his childhood.

The Cubs never again challenged for a pennant while Banks played. But his was the portrait of a happy man. Ernie Banks felt lucky. He was playing a game he loved, for a team he considered family, in a town that loved him back. There are some things in life more important than winning championships.

"Hey," said Ernie Banks, "what a beautiful day for baseball. Let's play two."

FUN

The New York Mets lost so many games in 1962 they were labeled baseball's worst team ever. They weren't so hot in 1963 either.

It was only June and the Mets were already fourteen games out of first place. Some players moped, taking the field with all the enthusiasm of a kid being sent to clean his room.

One steamy Sunday the Mets were playing the first game of a doubleheader against the lowly Philadelphia Phillies. The sparse crowd at the Polo Grounds was sleepy, just about yawning when Jimmy Piersall came to bat in the fifth.

Piersall, an unpredictable guy who once chased an umpire with a water pistol, was coming to the end of his colorful career.

He stepped into the batter's box against Dallas Green, the tall and serious Phillie hurler. Piersall got hold of a Green fastball and poked it over the outfield fence. It was his one-hundredth career home run. Maybe Hank Aaron and Babe Ruth wouldn't have been impressed but Piersall had a hankering to celebrate.

With a big smile on his face, Piersall watched the ball sail over the fence. Then he promptly did an about-face and began trotting to first base—backward!

The crowd went wild watching Piersall, now rounding second and third in this crazy backward home run trot, peering over his shoulder so he didn't trip over the bases. A bleak afternoon was suddenly a fun time at the oldball park.

Anyone who has ever played ball will tell you that winning is a great feeling. But in every game, one team's got to win while one team's got to lose. The happiest ball players are the ones who make up their minds to have fun, win or lose.

Take Steve Hamilton, a happy-go-lucky pitcher, tall in height and a little short on talent. On a muggy August afternonon at Yankee Stadium in 1970, the Bronx Bombers were playing the Cleveland Indians. It was a grim matchup of two sorry teams going nowhere. The Yanks were losing again when they called on Hamilton, their string-bean left-handed reliever, to mop up the game. No one at the park that day will ever forget what happened next.

The six-foot-seven Hamilton went into his windup against Cleveland slugger Tony Horton. Just before Hamilton was about to release the ball, he stopped. Ever so slowly Hamilton lofted the ball high into the air. It floated lazily toward Horton. They watched the pitch arc across home plate. A dumbfounded Horton froze.

"Strike one," cried the umpire as the ball settled into the catcher's mitt.

After a moment of disbelief, the crowd erupted in laughter and cheers. They had never seen a pitch so high and so slow.

Horton stared at Hamilton like he was looking at a Martian. Throw him one of those slow babies again and Horton figured to send it out of the park in a hurry.

Hamilton obliged.

He threw his "Folly Floater" once more and this time Horton was ready. He couldn't wait to get a hack at that fat, slow, ridiculous pitch. He uncorked a mighty swing and . . . and nothing. The ball barely ticked his bat, popping up in the infield for an easy out.

The father of the Folly Floater.

The crowd was howling. This time even Horton had to see the humor in it. He dropped to his knees and, on all fours, crawled back to his dugout. By the time he reached the dugout steps and waved a white towel of surrender, the entire stadium was in stitches.

The "Folly Floater" didn't change the course of baseball history, but it reminded players and fans that the game is supposed to be fun.

Still, baseball wasn't ready for The Bird. In 1976 a wiry rookie with the look of a scarecrow broke into the Detroit Tigers starting rotation. Detroit was a weak team that year but Mark Fidrych pitched twenty-four complete games, winning nineteen of them. He set the league on its ear with a very low 2.34 ERA.

But that's not what fans or ball players remember. Mark "The Bird" Fidrych would stand on the mound before each pitch and talk to the ball.

"Now, c'mon ball, be good. Don't get hit," he'd say.

At first other ball players were angry. They thought he was trying to show them up. But soon they came to realize that Fidrych was just a free spirit having a good time playing ball. He'd take the mound at Tiger Stadium as though he were having a catch with friends in his backyard. When the Tigers took the field he was the first one out, as if he were a kid and the first guy to the mound got to pitch.

Wherever and whenever he pitched, ballparks sold out. People said he was the best thing that happened to baseball in a long time.

But the very next season The Bird hurt his wing. He tried a few unsuccessful comebacks but his arm never came around. A few years later he was pumping gas for a living.

"Regrets?" he said. "No way. I had a ball."

So did Marv Throneberry. Maybe he didn't have all the talent in the world and, okay, so he couldn't catch a baseball to save his life, but the fans loved him. The thing is, Throneberry always tried so hard and it always seemed to come out so wrong.

He played in the perfect place for his talents, in a place where only he could thrive—first base for the helpless New York Mets. One time in 1963, Marvelous Marv, as the Mets fans called him, came to bat with two outs and a man on base. Somehow he got a hold of one and belted it into the outfield alley for extra bases. Did the slow-footed Throneberry ever run.

He churned around first. He huffed around second, finally plopping in at third base. Safely, he thought. But the infielder got hold of the ball and stepped on second base.

"You're out," the umpire yelled, pointing to Throneberry at third base. "You forgot to touch second base."

Throneberry's manager, old Casey Stengel, scrambled out of the dugout to argue the call and defend the Marvelous One.

"Don't bother, Casey," said the umpire. "He missed first base, too."

If anyone could laugh about that, it was Casey Stengel, the crinkled-faced man with a great sense of humor. He used laughter to ease the tension of a pennant race or to disarm a hostile crowd.

As a player for the Dodgers in 1919, Stengel had a horrible game at Ebbetts Field, in Brooklyn. The next day he returned to the ballpark and the crowd greeted him with boos and jeers. Casey faced the fans and bowed. Then he tipped his cap.

Out flew a sparrow. The crowd screamed and cheered.

Stengel didn't even mind it when, after the game, his manager said he always suspected that Casey was a birdbrain.

Even while managing the Yankees to five consecutive World Series titles from 1949 to 1953, Casey refused to take himself or the game of baseball too seriously.

Casey once sized up a hapless rookie this way: "He's only twenty years old. And in ten years he has a good chance of being thirty."

Then there was the time Casey went to the mound to replace a pitcher, and the player said, "I'm not tired." Stengel replied, "I'm tired of you."

The "Ol' Perfessor" never minded making a spectacle of himself.

But what Stengel may be best remembered for is his vague, bumbling, and unique language. It is now referred to as "Stengelese."

"I won't trade my left fielder," he told a writer.

"Who is your left fielder?" the reporter asked.

"I don't know," Casey said. "But if it isn't him, I'll keep him anyway."

Good luck figuring out what Casey meant. But remember, there is a place in baseball for fun.

That's something even the best of us forget sometimes.

Remember Jimmy Piersall, the guy who performed his home run trot backward? His manager got so ticked off at this horseplay that the very next day he cut Piersall from the team.

His manager was Casey Stengel.

CATCH WITHOUT END . . . AMEN

No one's gonna catch this one. . . . Big trouble . . . It's going toward the 475-foot sign in dead center. . . . This one's gonna score a . . . Wait a second. There goes Willie tearing after it. The ball's sailing over his head and . . .

He caught it. He caught it with his back to home plate. Unbelievable. Now he spins and he's falling but he hurls the ball back to the infield. What a throw. He stops the runner from scoring.

Wow! Willie Mays, out of nowhere, with his back to home plate, stole a sure triple from Vic Wertz and made a miraculous off-balance throw. No one scored. The game remains tied.

Remember this one, folks. This one was heaven-sent. Nobody but Willie Mays could have made that play.

If anyone is baseball's god of joy it's Willie Mays. The way he galloped around the bases. The waist-high basket catches he made. The spidery strides stretching a single into a double. The swing, a sudden explosion of energy, launching baseballs into the Pacific sunset.

His smile, a kid's smile—ear-to-ear. Because Willie Mays was in love with the game.

Willie was the guy who made the great catches at the Polo Grounds in World Series games. But he was also the man who, after the game, played stickball with kids in the poor neighborhood outside the ballpark.

Can you imagine? You're playing baseball with a broomstick and a rubber ball on a street crowded with parked cars. Suddenly the greatest player in baseball walks up to you and says, "Say, hey, can I play?"

If Willie Mays is baseball's god of joy, it's because he is the connection between major league stadiums and the playgrounds of America.

Baseball connects us all. Dig under the surface of any baseball story and its roots lead to another.

A baseball leaves the hand of Ken Griffey, Sr., and settles in the glove of Ken Griffey, Jr. A generation later the boy is a man and he climbs the outfield wall to make a great catch in Yankee Stadium, a place where almost thirty years earlier Roger Maris chased the ghost of Babe Ruth. It is the same place where a dying ballplayer named Lou Gehrig said he was the luckiest man on the face of the earth.

Across the street from the stadium was a ballpark where a kid named Moose Stubing chased his dream with the help of Lou Zaklin, his sandlot coach. Zaklin named himself after Lou Gehrig. And fifty years later Zaklin would lead a boy to a Bronx church to keep alive the memory of his hero. As in Brooklyn churches where old men still light candles for the memory of their hero, Gil Hodges.

Hodges was like the tree that grew in Brooklyn, tall and strong and patient. The tree of baseball is ringed with heroes and every generation adds branches. Suzyn Waldman was a little girl when she went to her first game at Boston's Fenway Park. She gasped

On the day of a big game at the Polo Grounds, superstar Willie Mays stops on a Harlem street to play stickball with neighborhood kids.

when she saw the chiseled face of the man in the on-deck circle. She turned to her grandfather and said, "If God is a person, that's what he looks like."

The little girl was speaking of Ted Williams. Waldman plucked from Williams his determination and single-mindedness and made it her own. She blazed a path for women in baseball broadcasting and millions heard her voice when, in 1989, she reported from the top of Candlestick Park that the earth was shaking.

She told of how her friend, Dave Stewart, who was pitching in that World Series, walked the streets of Oakland after the earthquake, how he helped the rescuers as they searched the rubble for survivors.

Stewart's compassion reminded people of Roberto Clemente, who died on a mercy flight to bring supplies to earthquake victims in Nicaragua. Baseball named its humanitarian award for Clemente. The summer after the Bay Area earthquake, Roberto Clemente's widow handed the award to Dave Stewart.

Baseball's roots nourished Jesse Barfield, the man who stood up for Suzyn Waldman's rights. Barfield learned to love the game sitting next to his aunt at Wrigley Field. She pointed out the joyful slugger Ernie Banks and together they cheered for him. And one day, after he became a major leaguer, he brought his son to a baseball-card show. He also met a friend there, Ken Griffey, Jr. Together they stood in line to get the autograph of one smiling old-timer named Ernie Banks.

It was an older Banks who consoled a young Mike Schmidt when the rookie could do nothing but strike out. Banks knew what it meant to have an old hand pat you on the back. Banks himself was encouraged by the old Negro League legend, Cool Papa Bell.

Cool Papa Bell is the patron saint of all the old ball players whose great hits and great catches were never chronicled but whose beauty is undiminished. Like the 1906 White Sox. They may be ancient history but every underdog that ever beat the big boys on the block is a part of that team, too.

What's the difference between the 1906 White Sox and the 1969 Mets but the passing of seasons? Long before the Mets played in Queens, it was home to two immigrant parents from Italy. Their boy, Mario Cuomo, played baseball for the Pittsburgh Pirates organization. The same scout who signed Moose Stubing signed Cuomo.

And if that boy, the future governor of New York, had continued playing ball, maybe he would have played center field next to Roberto Clemente.

Maybe he would have been there when Clemente belted his three thousandth and final hit on the last day of the 1972 season. Instead, Clemente was congratulated by the god of baseball joy, Willie Mays, who raced out of the opposing dugout to shake his hand.

Connected.

Just as Mays is connected to the kids he played stickball with, who are now fathers and grandfathers having a catch with their kids. The stickball and the players are all part of that same mighty tree. This is the joy of the game, an endless journey of a round ball in the eternal sky.

Deep to center. Mays is going back; he's racing for it.

That ball is going, going, and still going. . . .